OVER THERE

RACHEL WINDSOR

SAPPHIRE BOOKS

SALINAS, CALIFORNIA

Over There
Copyright © 2016 by Rachel Windsor. All rights reserved.

ISBN - 978-1-943353-55-2

This is a work of fiction - names, characters, places, and incidents are the product of the author's imagination or are used fictitiously. Any resemblance to actual persons living or dead, business, events or locales is entirely coincidental.

All rights reserved. No part of this publication may be reproduced, distributed, or transmitted in any form or by any means, including photocopying, recording, or other electronic or mechanical methods, without written permission of the publisher.

Editor - Kaycee Hawn
Book Design - LJ Reynolds
Cover Design - Michelle Brodeur

Sapphire Books Publishing, LLC
P.O. Box 8142
Salinas, CA 93912
www.sapphirebooks.com

Printed in the United States of America
First Edition - Dec. 2016

This and other Sapphire Books titles can be found at
www.sapphirebooks.com

OVER THERE

Dedication

For Gabby

Acknowledgment

As always, my first thank you goes to my wife, Gabby. As I think multiple times every day—lucky me.

Thank you to Chris and Schileen at Sapphire Books. What a privilege to work with this publishing house and these women.

To Michelle Brodeur for my all-time favorite cover design. The cover for this book is perfect in every way.

Thank you to Kaycee Hawn for your sharp eyes and keen editing. Now that I've had the pleasure of working with you, I can't imagine working without you.

To Lori Reynolds, my book designer. Once again, your style and skill allows my book to come out of the writing process looking amazing. Thank you.

Chapter One

Indiana had always seemed small and isolated to Ruth Carroway. At twenty years old and with a personality that her parents described with sometimes clenched teeth as "willful," Ruth did not intend to spend the rest of her life in the sleepy little town of Evansville. It just seemed to be taking longer than she had planned to find a way out. But on that Sunday in early December, never had her hometown seemed so close to the exotic island in the Pacific that they were talking about on the radio. Hawaii. Ruth repeated the name several times in her head. It even sounded exotic. But the endless news reports from Pearl Harbor were anything but.

Ruth and her older brother, Frank, crowded with their parents in the living room around the family's radio, listening with somber faces to the reports that had started at 1:30 that afternoon. The family had gathered after lunch to listen to a presentation on *Great Plays*, their usual Sunday tradition. What had started out as a promising entertaining program, a drama called "The Inspector General," had been interrupted suddenly by a frantic report from an on-site reporter in Hawaii. The report had seemed so unreal, so fantastic, that the four had looked at one another with raised eyebrows.

"What's this?" Pop had said around his pipe.

"Maybe a new program," Frank replied.

Ruth had scowled at Frank, a small gesture for

which she would later feel guilty. It was so like Frank to have an answer for everything. Before she could craft a retort, the reporter had continued.

The announcer sounded panicked and nearly breathless. "We have witnessed this morning the attack on Pearl Harbor and a severe bombing of Pearl Harbor by army planes, undoubtedly Japanese. The city of Honolulu has also been attacked and considerable damage done. This battle has been going on for nearly three hours…It's no joke; it's a real war."

The next several hours saw the Carroways glued to the radio, listening in disbelief. The family knew that whatever was happening around the world, so far from their safe little home in their safe little town, it was real. They had spent the rest of the afternoon listening to the reports, eager for more information and horrified at the same time. Mother had been crying since the beginning, her handkerchief soaked with tears and her eyes red.

"Those poor boys," she had repeated again and again.

The men of the Carroway family had reacted with a more aggressive stance.

"Sons of bitches!" Frank railed.

Mother removed her handkerchief long enough to scold her grown son. "Franklin!"

"He's right, dear. Cowardly Japs. Raining hell on the poor boys while they slept. That's not what soldiers do. We won't stand for this."

Neil Carroway had served in World War I, lying about his age, and seldom talked about it. Ruth had asked him about his experiences when she was younger, only to have her mother shoo her away. Her father hadn't reacted at all; he had only stared off at some unseen memory. She had never asked again.

"The President will take us into war, won't he, Pop?" Frank asked. His tone sounded hopeful.

"I don't see any other way, son. We're Americans. We can't let them get away with this."

Neil's pronouncement sent his wife into a fresh flurry of tears as she rushed into the kitchen. Everyone knew what she was thinking. Pop was likely not going anywhere, not with his bad leg and his age. But Frank... young, strong Frank was another story.

Ruth imagined her handsome brother in an Army uniform, marching off to war. It was hard to align the image with the constant presence in her life. She shook her head, warding off the thought.

Neil didn't follow his wife into the kitchen. It wasn't his way. Nor did Mary Carroway expect him to. His only nod to her sensitivity had been to hold back additional commentary on one particular detail on the attack while she was in the room. "Radio says many of the sailors burned alive."

Ruth's hands came to her mouth in horror. She shook away an unbidden image of sailors her age, on a burning ship, aflame and screaming for help that would never come.

The day wore on into evening. Everyone was restless but the routine of life played on. Dinner was prepared and the Carroways sat down for their evening meal, circling the pine table at which Ruth had eaten nearly every meal of her life. Neil said a simple prayer as he always did, but added an extra missive, one that would prove prophetic.

"And give our family strength for the changing times that will be coming our way."

Chapter Two

"And give our family strength for the changing times that will be coming our way." By April of 1942, things were indeed different for the Carroway family, as they were for the world.

"Are you scared?" Ruth fiddled with an old baseball as she sat on Frank's bed. Frank had sweated through his white tee shirt as he moved about his room, packing a footlocker.

"Sure."

"Why are you packing so many clothes? The Army will give you uniforms."

"I know that, knucklehead. I have to have something to wear during the trip, don't I?" Frank studied his packing. "Although, maybe you're right. I probably won't need this much." He extracted items, one by one, laying waste to the formerly neat trunk.

"Mom sure is a mess," Ruth said. It was an understatement. Ever since Frank had volunteered for duty, their mother had spent most of her time praying, and the time that she didn't spend praying, she spent crying.

Frank looked up. "I know." He frowned and shook his head. "I feel bad about it but I don't have a choice. I have to go. It's my duty."

Ruth nodded. Having grown up in a house with Neil Carroway, both she and her brother knew that there was no arguing with duty.

"You have a duty, too, you know." Frank resumed his work on the trunk.

"I know, make sure I'm the faithful daughter," Ruth said, her voice sarcastic.

"I'm serious. Mom needs you to be supportive, take over some of the things I do around the house. Dad, too."

Ruth knew Frank was right. She hated seeing her brother go but the feeling was layered. Frank was their mother's favorite. It was obvious despite Mary's efforts to assure Ruth that "no mother ever has a favorite." Truth be told, Frank was likely their father's favorite as well. He was the perfect son—smart, strong, handsome. He was a good boy, Mary had always said. And now he was a good man, marching off to war. Ruth had an instinct that Frank's wartime absence would make Mary's affection for her oldest even more pronounced, and where would that leave Ruth? The pesky younger sister, often an afterthought. A young woman who had never gone anywhere or done anything particularly special. She scolded herself silently. What was she doing being so selfish at a time like this?

"I'll tell you one thing, sis." Frank leaned in conspiratorially, his eyes sparkling with mischievousness. "Being short on the list to be sent over there has done wonders for my love life." He smiled broadly.

"What?"

"Girls are happy to give a soldier a fond farewell. And I do mean fond." Frank winked.

"Franklin Carroway! You're awful!" Ruth laughed, despite her words.

"That's not what the girls say." Frank narrowly avoided the pillow that Ruth threw at him. "But listen,

I don't want you being like the other girls. Don't let these fellows heading over there sweet talk you into... giving fond farewells." Frank's eyes were serious.

Ruth felt a mixture of pleasure that her brother cared about her and irritation that he was telling her what to do. It was her usual sentiment when it came to Frank. She pulled a face. "Don't worry. I have no interest in giving any boy a fond farewell or any other kind of farewell, for that matter."

Frank nodded, satisfied with the answer. He knew that the emphatic denial from his sister wasn't a pat protestation or for his benefit. Ruth had never been boy-crazy, unlike many of the girls in town. In fact, if Frank had been more observant, he might have realized that he needn't have bothered giving Ruth the talk because his sister appeared to be wholly uninterested in dating.

After removing another pair of trousers from his suitcase, Frank looked at Ruth. "How about this?"

Ruth nodded her approval. "Better. You have to be able to carry the thing, after all."

Frank leaned all of his weight on the case and snapped it shut. He patted it. "That should do it." He sat down on the bed, resting his elbow on the trunk.

Ruth drew her feet under her body and turned toward her brother. "What do you think it will be like?"

"I don't know. Dad talked to me the other day a little about his time in the Navy. It was mostly about the friends he made, though. He still didn't say much about the actual war."

"He never does. But I would have thought he might change that with you going away. You know, father/son stuff."

Frank nodded. "I thought so, too. I could have

asked, I guess, but you know how he is about that."

"I know. Do you think you'll be like that when you come back?"

Frank considered and stared at the ceiling for a moment before responding. "Hard to tell. Something made Dad that way. Maybe that's how everyone is when they come back."

Ruth traced an imagined pattern on the worn suitcase. "Maybe. But I want to know more about it when you're back. Do you promise to tell me everything?"

Frank laughed his easy laugh. "Promise."

The two siblings sat for a moment, each lost in their own thoughts. They were Neil Carroway's children and, because of that, had a bent toward internalizing things, even important things. Ruth did not plead with her brother to be careful and to make sure he did, in fact, come back. Frank did not tell Ruth that he loved her and wanted her to be strong if he didn't make it home. Even so, each was comfortable with the way they were leaving one another. Both knew, to some degree, what the other was thinking. Ruth broke the silence.

"So, which girls have been the fondest?" Ruth asked, her smile playful.

"A gentleman never kisses and tells."

Chapter Three

A paper map of the United States hung over Ruth's bed, held in place by pushpins and slightly curling at the corners. Ruth's goal was to travel to each of the forty-eight states. The map gave bleak testimony to her progress so far: exactly two. Indiana, of course, and a brief foray into the western part of Ohio to visit her mother's family when she was fifteen. Ruth lay on her bed, staring at the map and doing math in her head. *At this rate, I'll have to live to be almost 500 years old in order to see all of the states.*

Her room had become a place to escape the constant reminders of her brother's absence. Frank's room was exactly as it had been on the day he left, at Mary's insistence. Even a pair of shoes that Frank had left behind lay in the middle of the floor, a housekeeping slight that Mary normally never would have tolerated. Frank's conspicuous absence wasn't confined to his bedroom. Mary had created a shrine of sorts in the living room on a small table. The centerpiece was a large, framed picture of Frank on his high school graduation day. His favorite baseball glove, well-worn and the color of tobacco, rested alongside a school ribbon for a long-forgotten spelling bee. Mary kept the three letters that the family had received from Frank stacked on the table and neatly re-arranged them every time she re-read one, which was daily.

"You okay, dear?" Mary asked as she entered

with a load of clean laundry.

"Sure, Mom. Can I help you with that?"

Mary placed the laundry on Ruth's bed and sat down beside her daughter. "Just dropping off." She patted Ruth's leg. "Thinking about your brother?"

The truth was Ruth hadn't been thinking about Frank. She'd been wondering when she'd ever get to see the world. But that information would make her mother cross, so Ruth simply nodded.

"I've found that helping with the war effort gives me some comfort. I know it's for all of the boys over there, but in my mind, I'm doing something for just Frank. Does that make sense?"

Again, Ruth nodded. The family had been active in home front efforts, from Neil's victory garden (twice the size of anyone else on the block!) to Mary's tireless work coordinating rubber and tin drives. "That's a good idea. I can help you with the drives."

"I was thinking of something else for you. You know Lillian Reed two blocks over?"

Evansville was a small town and people Ruth's age tended to know one another. She was familiar with Lillian, having been in high school two years behind her. She knew that Lillian and her newlywed husband, Gerald, lived nearby and the women exchanged friendly waves when they saw one another. "Sure, but what's that got to do with helping out?"

Mary's face became animated, a welcome change from her worried countenance that had become near permanent since the start of the war. "Some of the girls and I have been working on a victory at home group, trying to support the younger women who are war brides. It can be so difficult for them, many newly married, some with babies, with their husbands called away. Lillian's husband, Gerald, is on the front and they've barely been married a year. It might be nice if you made a point to visit her often, make sure she's okay, that sort of thing."

Ruth thought that unsolicited visits from a woman who didn't understand what she was going through were likely the last thing that Lillian Reed wanted, but she didn't want to disappoint her mother. "That's a great idea. I'll stop by tomorrow."

Mary's smile was worth what Ruth expected to be an awkward, one-time inconvenience. "That's wonderful, dear. I imagine it will do you both some good."

※ ※ ※ ※

As soon as she knocked on the door to Lillian Reed's small but cozy home the next day, Ruth felt a stab of nervousness. Would Lillian think she was being intrusive? Why in the world would talking with a woman who she barely knew make her feel better about her husband being at war? Why had she let her mother talk her into this? Ruth fidgeted with the wrapped loaf of zucchini bread that Mary had insisted Ruth take with her.

The screen door swung open and Lillian Reed, twenty-two years old, blond-haired, and blue-eyed, confirmed Ruth's anxieties. She looked confused about Ruth's unexplained and uninvited presence on her porch.

"Hello?" Lillian asked, more of a question than a greeting.

Despite her suddenly dry mouth, Ruth heard herself speak. "Hi. I'm Ruth, Ruth Carroway from two blocks over. I, um, my mother volunteers with the war groups and thought it might be helpful if I stopped in."

Lillian stared at Ruth, an eyebrow raised.

Ruth felt her cheeks flame. "Not to presume I'd help you feel better, I mean, but more to...say hello." The words trailed off in an awkward cluster. She thrust the bread at Lillian, ready to make her escape.

When an understanding smile took over Lillian's face, her entire demeanor changed. With warm eyes and a look of relief, Lillian opened the door farther, beckoning Ruth in. "I'm so sorry; I'm being rude. I'm thrilled to have you for company. Please come in."

Ruth hesitated. It would be so much easier to drop the loaf into Lillian's hands and make a hasty exit. She would have done what her mother asked, technically, and could be on her way, free of this uncomfortable moment on the porch. But she didn't want to disappoint her mother. Besides, Lillian seemed happy enough to visit with her, so what was the harm? With a deep breath, she stepped over the threshold.

Lillian's home was different than Ruth had expected. It seemed so "grown-up," although when Ruth thought about it, why wouldn't it? Lillian was a married woman, after all. Although smaller than her parents' home, Lillian's nonetheless looked very similar. Tidy and efficient, it was obvious that Lillian spent much of her day making sure the house looked just so.

"Sit down," Lillian said, gesturing to the worn but clean couch.

"Thank you." Ruth sat as directed and noticed the phonograph on a nearby table. "You like music?"

Lillian smiled as she sat beside Ruth. "Absolutely love it. You?"

"Sure."

"Sometimes I'll put on a record and just dance by

myself. I know that's silly."

Ruth shook her head, anxious to put Lillian at ease despite being a bit nervous herself. "No, it's not. I like to do that, too. You don't have to think or worry about anything when you're dancing." She blushed as soon as her words were out. Lillian had just been making conversation and Ruth had gotten too serious, too intimate. To her surprise, Lillian lit up.

"I know just what you mean." Lillian situated herself so that she was facing Ruth on the couch and touched Ruth's leg to emphasize her point. "It's your own little world. Well, for at least as long as the song lasts."

Ruth laughed, mostly to distract herself from the warm feeling she was getting from Lillian's hand being on her leg. Lillian was so tall and beautiful that she made Ruth feel like a discomfited teenager, despite the slight age difference between them. And she truly was beautiful. With long legs and perfect skin, Lillian looked like a movie star. Her eyes were a pale blue, almost translucent. Ruth could feel herself gaping. She realized she was staring and forced herself to look away. Why was she acting this way around Lillian, anyhow?

"It must be tough," Ruth said, "Having your husband away at war."

Lillian nodded, her head bobbing so hard that her pin curls bounced. "It's terrible. I miss Gerald awfully and of course, I worry. I try not to read the papers because it makes me even more nervous for him but in the end, I can't keep myself away."

"My brother is over there, too. Frank?"

"I know Frank. He's a good fellow."

"I worry about him; we all do. But I guess it's probably different when it's your husband." Ruth made eye contact with Lillian and felt those blue eyes pulling her in again. Something about the way that Lillian looked at her made her feel good—understood and interesting.

"I get scared a lot," Lillian confessed, fidgeting with the hem of her skirt and not looking at Ruth.

Ruth nodded. "About Gerald?"

"Gerald, yes, of course. I meant about being here by myself. It sounds silly, I know, but at night, I get nervous. I've never lived by myself in my whole life. Lots of sounds after the sun goes down, I guess." She laughed self-consciously, stealing a glance at Ruth to see how she was receiving her revelation.

Ruth leaned forward. "Doesn't sound silly at all. I know I'd get spooked if I lived by myself. It must be so different, being by yourself, I mean."

Lillian exhaled. "Oh, it is. I thought you'd laugh at me for being a scaredy-cat. It does get scary sometimes, though, and lonesome."

The idea sprang from Ruth's lips before it had fully coalesced in her mind. "We should be roommates!" The suggestion sounded so inappropriate and bold that Ruth actually brought her hands to her mouth after she spoke, as if to return the words to where they came from. "I'm sorry, that was so—"

"No!" Lillian clapped her hands merrily. "I love the idea! I would so enjoy the company."

"You would?" Ruth was surprised, and relieved that she hadn't made a fool of herself.

"Oh, yes. I know I should be able to make it on my own, especially with the things people are going through all over the world, but having a friend here would make it so much easier."

Ruth's face warmed when she heard Lillian refer

to her as a friend. "It's settled then. Roommates!"

Lillian leaned forward and hugged Ruth impulsively. "Can you move in today?"

☙☙❦❦

Once the idea had taken shape, the women put it into action immediately. While not the same day as Lillian had suggested, the next morning saw Ruth carrying her suitcase to the other woman's home. After several trips with boxes, she had moved her life to the neat little house.

"Move in?" her mother had said. "I sent you over just to visit." The sudden change in plans had taken Mary aback when Ruth excitedly told her parents the plan the day before.

"I know, but once we got to talking, it just seemed like a good idea. Lillian needs the company and it's a way for me to help."

Ruth knew which words would smooth the news and anything to do with helping the war effort was top of that list. She was right.

"I suppose so. It's very generous of you, Ruth."

That night, lying in her bed, Ruth could hardly sleep. The newness of the adventure, even if it was just moving in with a new friend in the neighborhood, was the most interesting thing that had happened to her for a very long time. Even though it wasn't her own house, of course, moving away from her parents made her feel like an adult, as if a new phase of her life was beginning.

But there was something else keeping her awake. Ruth found herself thinking back to her conversation with Lillian earlier, the way Lillian looked at her and touched her leg when she got animated. More importantly, Ruth couldn't stop thinking about how Lillian had made her feel. Now if she could only figure out what that meant.

Lillian greeted her at the door like an old friend. "I'm so glad you're here!" she exclaimed when Ruth arrived with the first load. "Let me take that."

In less than an hour, the two women had unpacked all of Ruth's things and Lillian had given Ruth the grand tour. They spent the day talking, laughing, and working in Lillian's large vegetable garden. Mealtime went smoothly, with Lillian cooking and Ruth cleaning, both falling into an easy, comfortable rhythm.

"It's as if we've always known each other," Ruth said after the two settled down from yet another laugh.

"Isn't it? It's wonderful already. I didn't realize how lonely I had been."

That night, after the dinner dishes had been put away and the radio had been turned off, Ruth knocked on Lillian's bedroom doorframe. "Just wanted to say goodnight."

Lillian was sitting in her bed, reading a book. She looked up and frowned. "No! Not yet. Let's talk some more."

Ruth laughed as she walked in. "Aren't you talked out yet?"

Lillian patted the bed beside her. "Never. You don't know what you've gotten yourself into, Ruth."

The two laughed and giggled well into the night, gossiping about neighbors, classmates from high school, and occasionally delving into the serious with worries about the war and Frank and Gerald. When the sun rose, the two were curled up in Lillian's bed, having fallen asleep before Ruth made it to the guest room. It was a new day.

Chapter Four

The first few weeks that the women had lived together had felt like a lark, like schoolgirls spending the night. But as time wore on, they had developed routines and roles. Ruth liked how it felt. They existed comfortably alongside each other, sharing stories and thoughts. Lillian told Ruth more than once that she was very happy with the arrangement and that she felt much better with Ruth there. Mary seemed proud of Ruth and Ruth enjoyed being with Lillian. For wartime, it was as happy a time as one could hope for.

The two had divided up the household chores and Ruth approached hers with a vigor not seen when she did chores at her "own" house. One afternoon, Ruth struggled with heavy bedding, removing it from a clothesline. It smelled clean and fresh from being hung outside. Ruth buried her nose in a sheet and inhaled deeply, enjoying the scent. After finally managing everything into an approximate folded bundle, she carried it inside.

Lillian looked up from the kitchen table where she was shelling peas. "Oh, aren't you a sweetheart for doing that! Thank you."

"It's no trouble." Ruth felt a small flush of pleasure at the compliment from Lillian. There was something else, though. She rested the bundle on the table. "I have some big news."

"Something bad? Has something happened?" Lillian looked stricken. As a wartime wife, any news could be assumed to be bad news.

Ruth saw the fear on her friend's face and immediately felt badly. "No, no! Nothing bad. It's good news."

Lillian breathed out a sigh of relief and returned to the peas. "Thank goodness! Well, spit it out, you look like you're about to burst."

Ruth laughed. "I guess I am. I got a job."

"A job?"

"Yes. At the factory. I'll be a riveter on the aircraft line. I'll be helping the boys overseas." Ruth had applied for the job on a lark, never expecting to be hired. What would the factory need with a young girl like her, anyway? As it turned out, the factory needed everyone it could get its hands on and Ruth was hired on the spot.

"That's wonderful!" Lillian's smile immediately fell.

"What's wrong?"

"Oh, it's nothing. Just being silly."

"Tell me."

Lillian pushed the peas away. "I'm being terribly selfish but I just was thinking if you're at work all day, I'll miss you. I'll miss having you here with me." She looked up at Ruth, gauging her reaction.

Ruth felt a warm, pleasant feeling wash over her. It was powerful. "I'll miss you, too, I really will."

An awkward silence fell. Finally, Ruth picked up the bundle once more. "Where should I put these?"

"The closet in the guest room if you can squeeze it in there." Lillian gave Ruth a smile.

Inside the small extra bedroom, Ruth laid the

blankets on the lumpy bed, exhaling as she released the burden. Wiping a small bead of sweat from her brow, she opened the closet to see if she could find a home for her load. The little space smelled faintly of mothballs and offered little hope of containing the bedclothes.

Ruth frowned at the row of Gerald's clothing, hanging from the rod. She looked at the door before touching a few of the shirts. His presence was strong here and even though it was his house, he seemed like an intruder. Ruth shook her head. *I'm being silly*, she told herself. Gerald was halfway across the world, serving his country. She was the intruder, not him. She was just a guest here, she reminded herself. Just a guest.

Ruth knelt down to see if the bedding would fit at the bottom of the closet. Gerald's bowling ball took a prized spot, as did several pairs of his shoes. Ruth looked again toward the door before removing a pair of chestnut wingtips. The shoes were huge, even bigger than Frank's, and highly shined. She took off her own oxfords and slid on the larger shoes. Holding one foot out for examination, Ruth giggled. She kept them on as she continued to look for a place for the bedding. A cardboard box in the back of the closet occupied a space that looked promising. Ruth pulled the box out and gasped when it tipped over.

Inside the box were dozens of pin-up magazines, or "nudie magazines," as she had heard boys call them. Ruth gaped. She'd heard about these kinds of magazines but had certainly never seen one. She was absolutely positive that her father would never look at such a thing and although her brother Frank might be interested, Ruth guessed that fear of his mother catching him overshadowed any physical desire he had to look at a magazine like that. Even a young man of twenty-two would not want to face the wrath or worse, disappointment, of Mary Carroway.

In Lillian's house, apparently, there was no such fear of detection. Gerald's stash had been stowed in the closet, of course, but only in a box and not even a securely closed one at that. Ruth looked again from the pile of magazines, with their covers full of women and legs galore, to the door. Her curiosity got the best of her. Still wearing Gerald's too-big shoes, she clomped to the door and shut it quietly.

The first magazine Ruth grabbed was an eye-opener. Its cover featured a stunning redhead. To Ruth, the woman seemed to be all breasts and legs, but she supposed that was the idea. It was, after all, a pin-up magazine. She took a long look at the woman. She didn't look like the women around Evansville, that was for sure. No, the women in Evansville didn't wear clothes that showed off their long, supple legs, all the way to the hint of their privates like this woman did. Nor did they wear tops that strained to contain their breasts or showed their nipples, erect enough to poke just slightly through the material.

By now, Ruth was holding the magazine very close to her face, mesmerized. She knew what the magazine was selling and, by deduction, what the women of Evansville were decidedly not exuding. Sex. She hadn't ever seen a woman with such raw sexual appeal, one so openly displaying her body with pride. The woman on the cover knew she was gorgeous and knew she would turn a man wild with that body. Her confident posture and gaze, even through a picture, made her even more beautiful. Ruth was spellbound. She traced a long leg on the cover, starting at the model's high heel and gliding all the way up, finally hovering at her panty area.

She exhaled at last, finally realizing that she had been holding her breath. A warm flush washed over her and she recognized the sensation: arousal. Her knees wavered a bit with the realization and she sat down, right there at the foot of Lillian and Gerald's guest room closet, the bowling ball a silent witness.

Ruth fanned herself with the magazine, the very instrument of her own excitement. She looked at the cover again. Yes, it was the same. The woman appealed to Ruth with more than a woman's admiration for another's beauty. A nascent throb between her legs and an untouched longing told Ruth it was much more. Ruth felt raw desire and sexual attraction when she looked at the cover. The woman's feminine curves stirred in her feelings that she had always suspected but never explored. She swallowed hard as her body registered all of the things that her brain was still trying to catch up to.

Am I one of "those" girls? she wondered. Staring at the sexy two-dimensional temptress on the cover, she already knew the answer. The few times she had allowed the boys she had gone out with to touch her breasts while they kissed had done nothing for her physically, not even the time she let Andy go under her bra. And she certainly had felt nothing more than boredom and a hint of revulsion the time that she had permitted Andy (who had been so sweet and seemed so earnest) to place her hand on his pants over his bulging crotch. Yet here she was, in a full-fledged state of erotic readiness, simply from seeing a woman posing provocatively.

With a loud sigh, Ruth lay back on the floor and closed her eyes. There was more, she knew. These months with Lillian…being so close to her all of the time. Seeing her come out of the shower in just a towel, sitting together on the couch reading during the evening and, of course, the nights spent in the same bed. The feelings she was having for Lillian had eclipsed those of a solicitous friend long ago. She just hadn't known what to do about it. Clutching the magazine to her chest and feeling her heart beat not only in her chest but also below her waist, Ruth resolved to take action.

"What in the world are you doing?"

Opening her eyes, Ruth saw Lillian looking at her upside down.

Lillian stood in the now-opened door and stared at her roommate with a quizzical expression. She certainly had not expected to find Ruth wearing her husband's shoes, holding a girlie magazine, and lying on the floor. She wondered if Ruth had gone slightly mad. "Are you all right?" she asked as she kneeled beside Ruth. She put a hand on Ruth's forehead. "You're burning up!"

Ruth scrambled to her feet. "You startled me. I'm fine, just fine. I was looking for a place to put the bedding and got distracted."

Lillian surveyed the scene and nodded, a smile on her lips. "I can see that." She gently pulled the magazine from Ruth's hands. "Gerald's pin-up magazines?" With a raised eyebrow at Ruth, she flipped through the pages. "I never understood why he bought these, you know. I got so jealous."

Relieved that Lillian didn't seem to be horrified at Ruth's indiscretion, Ruth sat on the edge of the guest bed and patted the spot beside her. "Jealous?"

Lillian sat. "Sure. Who wouldn't be if their husband was spending time mooning over other women? Practically naked other women, I might add. It made me feel like…oh, I don't know. It's dumb, I guess." Her eyes welled up.

"No, it's not. Go on, tell me what you were going to say," Ruth urged, placing a hand on Lillian's leg.

"I'm being selfish. Gerald is across the world at war and here I am pouting like a jealous school girl."

Ruth rubbed Lillian's leg. "You're entitled to have feelings even while there's a war going on, Lil."

Lillian looked at Ruth and nodded, her tears now spilling over. Ruth used her thumb and wiped at the tears, being as gentle as she could.

"When he looked at those magazines," Lillian said, her voice rough with emotion, "I just felt like I wasn't enough for him. Like I wasn't exciting or beautiful like those girls." She nodded her head toward the closet where the cardboard box held all of her insecurities.

Ruth felt a flash of anger towards Gerald for making his wife feel even an instant of hurt or pain. Her focus quickly returned to the woman sitting so close to her that she could smell the Dove soap on her skin. She took Lillian's face in both hands and took a deep breath. She knew this was a turning point.

"Listen to me. You're an absolutely beautiful, exciting, and amazing woman. Any man… or woman who can't see that is a fool." Ruth didn't wait for a reaction. She listened to her heart and kissed Lillian gently, but fully, on the lips. To her surprise, Lillian kissed her back.

The women separated and looked at one another. Nervous, Lillian giggled and stood up. "That's the kind of pep talk I needed. Thank you, hon." With that, she stepped out of the room, leaving Ruth in her wake.

The rest of the afternoon and evening was stilted and awkward. Ruth cursed herself time and time again for her actions. The women had exchanged small talk over dinner and done the clean-up in virtual silence. Ruth found herself near tears by the time it was over. Making an excuse to retire early, she left the kitchen. Unsure of whether to sleep in Lillian's room given the day's events, she decided to continue as she had been, rather than make things even more uncomfortable.

Lying in the bed, she replayed the events again. Despite the repercussions, the moment when she realized that Lillian was kissing her back had been momentous. In that instant, Ruth knew she was indeed *one of those girls*. She smiled in the twilight. Her smile vanished as she heard Lillian's footsteps approach. She closed her eyes and pretended to be asleep. The women would have to talk about what happened, but it wouldn't be tonight. Ruth just didn't have the courage and from how dinner had gone, it didn't appear that Lillian did either.

Ruth kept her eyes shut as Lillian opened and closed dresser drawers. After a moment, there was no more movement but Ruth knew that Lillian had not yet joined her in the bed. *Had she gone to the guest room?* Risking being caught, Ruth opened her eyes. She wasn't expecting what she saw.

Lillian was standing beside the bed, her tall body clothed not in her usual long nightgown but instead in simply a bra and underwear. She stood on one tiptoe, a finger in her mouth, looking at Ruth expectantly.

Ruth stared. She had seen Lillian in various stages

of undress during their time together as roommates but nothing quite like this. Lillian's body was stunning, tall and womanly, with inviting hips and breasts virtually spilling over the cups of her brassiere. Her blonde pin curls were loose, giving her a wild look. But what struck Ruth the most was Lillian's expression. Lillian wanted Ruth's sexual affirmation. In a split second, Ruth realized that she had misread Lillian's tension throughout the afternoon. She hadn't regretted their moment in the guest room. Instead, it had unlocked in her something that now needed to be explored.

With a single finger, Ruth traced a line from Lillian's knee up to her panties. She stopped there and looked at Lillian. She knew this moment was important.

"You are the most exciting woman in this world, Lillian Reed. No pin-up girl could make me feel this way."

Lillian's smile spoke of relief and eager anticipation. "And what way is that?" she asked. The words were bold but her tone was not. It was clear that teasing in this way was foreign to Lillian.

Still looking at Lillian's body, as if unable to believe that what was happening was happening, Ruth dragged her finger past Lillian's cotton underwear and across her bare stomach. "Like my heart is about to come out of my chest. Like my privates are telling me where they are and what to do. Like I'm afraid this might be a dream." Finally, Ruth met Lillian's eyes. "Like I just came alive for the first time."

Lillian nodded. She knew what Ruth meant. Her body was reacting the same way. Her mind was racing with the implications of what this meant—after all, she was a married woman. But she couldn't overcome what she was feeling in the moment. The truth was, she didn't even want to try.

"I've never seen you like this," Ruth said unnecessarily.

Lillian giggled. "I wouldn't think so. I'm glad you like it. Seeing you look at me like that..."

Sitting up at last, Ruth furrowed a brow. "I'm sorry. I didn't mean to stare. Did I make you uncomfortable?"

"No, no. The opposite." Lillian was blushing now. "It makes me feel sexy, exciting. I like how you're looking at me."

"Thank God," Ruth said with a long exhale. "If you had told me not to look, I don't know if I could have done what you asked. You're just too beautiful." She swung her legs over the edge of the bed so that she faced Lillian. With a tentativeness borne of both inexperience and fear of rejection, Ruth placed her hands on Lillian's hips. The warm softness felt natural and welcoming. Reaching down, she ran her hands along the length of Lillian's legs, feeling their strong muscles and delighting in the freedom of touching this woman.

Lillian shivered. She was amazed at how her body was reacting to something as simple as a touch along her legs. She was very close to asking Ruth to touch her "down there." That was something she never felt with Gerald. Aware that her breathing was becoming heavy, Lillian stroked Ruth's dark hair slowly.

Ruth felt Lillian's gentle touch and closed her eyes automatically. The sensual stroking was the most erotic thing that Ruth had experienced in her young life. The realization that she was about to experience lovemaking with a woman enhanced the moment beyond words. She leaned forward and kissed Lillian's bare stomach. The first taste of her skin made Ruth suddenly ravenous for more.

Without preface, Ruth stood up, edging Lillian just far enough away so that Ruth could stand in front of her. "I want you." The words were brave and for Ruth, exhilarating.

Lillian held Ruth's gaze as she unfastened her brassiere. Once removed from her body, Lillian dropped the bra to the floor and stood before Ruth, offering herself.

The sight of Lillian's bare breasts, full and heavy with dark pink nipples that were hard with arousal, set Ruth free. *Yes*, she thought. *This is what I want.* Her hands went immediately to Lillian's breasts, feeling their heft, caressing the impossibly soft undersides, and gently rolling her nipples between thumbs and fingers. The physical effect on each woman was immediate and pronounced.

Lillian, who had more sexual experience with men, instantly knew that this was a different experience from those she had had with her husband or her one lover before Gerald. The men had pawed at her breasts, clearly a prelude for the main act. Ruth's sensual touches and attention to her nipples stirred a deeper arousal between Lillian's legs than she had ever felt before. Her breathing was fast and her eyes closed with pleasure.

For Ruth, the first touch of a woman electrified her body. She felt her own nipples harden, as if she was the one being fondled. She became intensely aware of the need between her legs as she pulsed. Her heart was racing and she heard the soft murmurs of appreciation that she was making without even being aware of it. Emboldened, she kissed Lillian. But this kiss was different from the one they had shared earlier that day. This kiss brought with it the passion and confidence that had been lacking. Ruth kept her hands on Lillian's breasts, kneading and pulling and teasing, as her mouth claimed Lillian's.

Lillian held Ruth's head, twisting her fingers in her hair as she opened herself to the kiss. Thrilling in the intensity of the connection, Lillian poked her tongue in Ruth's mouth and was pleased when she felt Ruth accept it. The women stood locked in an embrace, joined at the mouth, seemingly suspended in time.

When they finally broke, Ruth spoke. "I didn't know it would be like this." Her hungry eyes and flushed cheeks told Lillian that what they were experiencing was new to her as well.

"Can I undress you?" Lillian asked. She wanted to see Ruth, to touch her.

Ruth nodded.

Lillian slowly unbuttoned Ruth's pajama top and slid it off of her. When she reached down to remove Ruth's pajama pants, never breaking eye contact, Ruth whimpered.

"Is this okay?" Lillian asked.

Ruth could only nod, her breath coming so fast that she was afraid to speak.

The pants slid down to the floor with a little help from Lillian to push them past Ruth's buttocks. Lillian's hands paused on Ruth's rear, briefly but long enough to further excite them both.

The women faced one another, each clad only in their underwear. Lillian touched Ruth between the legs, lightly, drawing a groan from Ruth. "You're wet down there," Lillian said.

With a grin, Ruth touched Lillian's crotch. "So are you. Should we take these off?"

Lillian blushed. Despite what they were doing, she felt embarrassed suddenly. "Not tonight."

Ruth nodded. She needed no explanation. She couldn't keep her eyes from Lillian's body. A woman's body like her own, of course, but so different, so inviting.

Lillian dragged the edge of her hand between Ruth's legs.

"Oh my God," Ruth said, as her knees grew weak. "I have to lie down or I'll fall down." With that, she backed into the bed and lay down.

Lillian wasted no time in positioning herself beside her new lover. She returned her hand between Ruth's legs and began to rub deliberately up and down, with slow, languorous strokes. When Ruth let her legs fall open for Lillian, Lillian buried her face in Ruth's neck. Hearing Ruth's heavy breathing and moans of pleasure in her ear, Lillian responded by pressing harder.

"Oh, Lillian. Please keep going." Ruth's eyes were shut tight and she arched her hips upward.

The women pressed their bodies together, with Lillian rubbing Ruth's sex quickly through her wet underwear and Ruth's body going so fast that her mind could not keep up.

When Ruth's climax approached, she cried out, startled by the intensity of the exploding rings of pleasure. In that moment, she felt completely free, completely sexual, completely female. She trembled and arched repeatedly, giving herself over to the sensation and to Lillian.

When it was over, the women smiled at one another. No words were needed or shared. Lillian's need took over. She mounted Ruth and spread her legs over one of Ruth's muscular thighs before instinctually clamping her legs together, reveling in the pressure against her sex. When she felt Ruth's hands grasp her hips, her body took over. Grinding and pushing rhythmically into Ruth's leg, Lillian gasped. "Oh God." Ruth's grip tightened on her hips and Lillian moved in time with a raw drive and need that she had never before experienced.

Ruth looked up at Lillian's face. Lillian's eyes were closed and her lips were parted. In another context, it may have appeared that she was praying, supplicant to the heavens. But the context was clear. Lillian needed and wanted what Ruth had to give. The realization that their sexual arousal was shared linked the women, physically and emotionally. Ruth flexed her thigh and pushed into Lillian's wetness, sensing that she wanted more of her against her.

Ruth was right. Lillian responded readily to the offer by clamping even more tightly against Ruth's leg and increasing the tempo of her riding movements. A sudden bolt of exquisite pleasure gripped Lillian and she cried out. Jealously guarding the feeling and staying in the same position to ensure its continuation, Lillian felt her body floating away from her, with successive waves of white hot pleasure coursing through her. "Ruth," she moaned as she let the feeling take over.

They slept in one another's arms that night, not speaking or deconstructing what had just happened to them. The contentment they both felt was a delicious revelation. Lying just beneath the contentment were flames of desire, now stoked and impossible to ignore.

Chapter Five

Work at the factory turned out to be less exciting than Ruth had expected. The work was hard, detailed, and monotonous. Ruth's body was sore every day when she returned home, but she felt herself growing stronger. In any event, the satisfaction of doing a good job and doing her part for the country more than made up for the tough parts. Plus, she had made lots of new friends, mostly women who now made up the majority of the factory's workforce.

Ruth put her lunch pail in the small locker and saw Mary Ellen enter the break room.

"Morning," Mary Ellen said with a bright smile.

"Good morning." Something about Mary Ellen made Ruth feel that she might be a lesbian, but she couldn't quite place it and didn't dare ask. Mary Ellen held Ruth's eyes longer than other women did and Ruth met the gaze. As far as Ruth knew from small-town chatter, Mary Ellen not only wasn't married but also had never had a steady boyfriend.

"How are you, doll?" she asked as she stowed her lunch and began pulling her hair back in a handkerchief. All of the women wore their hair that way. The factory was dirty and loose, making long hair a safety hazard.

That was the other thing that Ruth thought was odd. Mary Ellen called all of the women at the plant "doll." Ruth liked it. Even though Mary Ellen called everyone doll, Ruth liked how it made her feel when she was the subject of the endearment.

"Fine, just fine. A little tired, I guess. I didn't sleep much last night." Ruth immediately regretted the words once they were out of her mouth. They were true, of course. She hadn't slept much the night before. Neither had Lillian. Now that they had discovered lovemaking, they were finding that they could scarcely wait until bedtime to climb under the covers and, once there, that they could scarcely leave one another alone long enough to go to sleep. Numerous nights had seen them scramble into bed well before the sun had set.

Mary Ellen closed her locker door and looked at Ruth, examining her face. "Is that right? You look pretty good to me for being tired. In fact, you sort of look like you're glowing."

Ruth felt her cheeks flame. She was sure that Mary Ellen knew exactly why she was tired. It was as if her nighttime pursuits with Lillian were written all over her forehead, a scarlet letter even more dramatic than Hawthorne's and one that this small town would never understand. But Mary Ellen did. That was clear now.

Mary Ellen held Ruth's chin in her hand briefly. "Good for you, doll. Just be careful. People around here won't take kindly to a soldier's wife with one of us."

Ruth was so shocked at being so easily identified that she could only nod her head mutely.

With that, Mary Ellen walked out of the break room, tossing a happy "hi, doll" to another woman who was coming in for the morning.

"Hi there, Ruth," the new arrival said. It was Cora York, a friendly girl who Ruth had gone to high school with. Her husband was at sea but that didn't stop Cora from having a bubbly attitude. Ruth wondered sometimes if Cora was in denial about the dangers her husband was facing.

"Morning, Cora. Ready for another day?"

"Sure am. Those aircraft wings won't make themselves."

Ruth smiled. She had shared the same exchange numerous times and each time Cora delivered her line with the same cheerful happiness.

Her tone didn't change despite the ugly words that came next, however. "I saw that Mary Ellen just now. You know what the girls say about her, don't you?" Cora didn't wait for an answer from Ruth. She was too anxious to share the news. "They say she's a lesbian. You know...she likes girls."

Ruth stared. "Who says that?"

Cora shrugged and pushed her blonde hair under her handkerchief. "Lots of the women on the rivet line. Susan said she heard that Mary Ellen actually made a *pass* at one of the new girls. Can you imagine?"

Ruth shut the locker door with a deliberate click. "Maybe you shouldn't listen to gossip, Cora. Or spread it."

Friendly Cora was not used to being scolded. She frowned at Ruth and went on the defensive. "Well, you seem awfully quick to stick up for her, Miss Carroway. Interesting." She shut her locker and strode toward the door. "I'll have to ask the other girls why they think that is."

The not so veiled threat hung ugly in Cora's wake, leaving Ruth to face dueling emotions. As quickly as she had been introduced and tacitly welcomed into a community where she might actually belong at last, she had learned first-hand just how unwelcome that community was in Evansville.

Ruth's mind was filled with thoughts of the breakroom encounter. The monotonous routine of the work did little to stop the replaying of the scene from the breakroom. She couldn't get over how quickly Cora's tone had changed—from pleasant banter to judgmental threats. Why? Ruth knew that people didn't talk openly about girls like her or Mary Ellen, but was it so terrible to be this way? What was it about liking other women that made others so uneasy, so mean? Cora knew Ruth from high school; she knew Ruth was a good person. She hadn't changed because she was falling in love with Lillian. Actually, Ruth knew, she had changed. She was happy and free at last. Those were good things, weren't they? Things that a friend would wish for another friend.

She tried to focus on her task, riveting endless bolt after bolt into the large piece of metal at her station. The heavy steel drill was warm in her hands, having been used non-stop since the beginning of Ruth's shift. She could feel her hands sweating inside of the thin gloves that she wore, a combination of the drill, exertion, and the gloves themselves. The drone of the drill, interrupted for just a moment when she moved to the next spot, was usually comforting to Ruth. Today, it was annoying. The smell of metal and the vibration of her body from the drill were making her queasy.

Ruth looked down the assembly line, watching her co-workers, all female, do the same job that she was doing. Their brows were furrowed in concentration, making sure that they put the holes in just the right spot; otherwise, the metal wings and other pieces destined for an aircraft would be rendered useless. Most women wore their hair up, layered under handkerchiefs or other wraps. All of the women had developed strong muscles in their arms from holding the drill eight or more hours per day. Ruth's own arms had gone from slightly flabby to toned and sinewy since she started at the factory. She knew Lillian liked it and smiled to herself as she remembered Lillian's words from the night before, when Ruth had held herself up, on top of Lillian as they moved together.

You're so strong. So powerful. I love watching you. The words had sent both of them into a frenzy of passion, pushing and thrusting into one another, aching for the release that made them both cry out with pleasure. Ruth blushed at the memory, simultaneously feeling her body react to the memory in other ways. She glanced at the line. Could the women read her mind? Did they know? Was it Ruth's imagination or were the women on the line looking at her, whispering their judgments? She could hardly wait to get home.

≈≈≈≈

Ruth stopped at her parents' home before going on to Lillian's. She had tried to make it a point to see them every day, to help with any tasks around the house that needed to be done and to share some of the emotional burden of Frank's absence. The visits were turning into a chore, however. Ruth was growing slowly to resent her mother's dead stare, her seeming inability to find anything at all to be happy about. It was taking a toll on her father, too. He tried very hard to cheer up his wife, to take her mind from the dangers Frank was facing. It was an impossible job rendered all the more difficult by Neil's personality.

Neil was a quiet man and not prone to shows of emotion. In his heart, he knew his wife was in pain, but he couldn't quite find the ways to connect with her to be of any comfort. Fixing a squeaky door or folding the newspaper neatly after reading it were his awkward attempts to make life easier for his wife but they did little to break through the sorrow and worry that filled Mary's days and nights. He had become impatient with her frequent initiation of conversation speculating about where Frank was at any given moment or what he was feeling. The speculations quickly grew morbid and dark and Neil wasn't interesting in playing the depressing parlor game that wasn't really a game. He had seen war and he had no problem envisioning what his son was going through. His only problem was trying not to envision those things.

"Hello there, stranger," Neil said with a warm smile when Ruth walked into the living room. Neil was sitting in his favorite chair, re-reading the day's news.

Ruth planted a kiss on her dad's head. "Hi, Pop."

"Your mother will be happy to see you."

With a sigh, Ruth looked toward the kitchen where she was mostly certain that her mother was moving about. "I know I've missed a couple of days…" The truth was it had been four days since she'd last visited, despite being just two streets over. It was next to impossible to tear herself away from Lillian. Even when they were just sitting together, listening to the radio, or preparing a meal together, her presence was intoxicating. The thought of leaving Lillian and ignoring the constant state of physical arousal that Ruth was experiencing to spend time in her parents' now depressing house had made the choice too easy.

Guilt had propelled her to her parents' house after work and she had guilt about that as well.

"You're busy; we understand." Neil folded up the paper and leaned forward in his chair. "You're doing good work at the factory, sweetie. It's something to be proud of." He looked at his daughter. "Something on your mind?"

Ruth looked again toward the kitchen and decided to confide in her father. "It seems like all Mom cares about is Frank. I know that sounds selfish and I feel terrible saying that. But she doesn't think my work is important. And she seems irritated with me all of the time."

"Your mother is very worried about Frank. We all are. It's just that her way of dealing with him being gone is different from ours. That's all."

Before Ruth could respond, her mother appeared.

"Thought I heard you. Are you staying for dinner?" Mary's voice was flat and her eyes held little warmth for her daughter.

Ruth tried not to take the coolness personally. She knew her mother was suffering. "No, not tonight. I'm pretty tired from the factory." Ruth hoped that the mention of her wartime efforts would lessen the sting of another refusal to linger at her home.

Mary nodded, wordlessly.

Neil, uneasy in his own house, cleared his throat. "I was just telling Ruth how proud we are of her work at the factory. It helps all of the boys."

Mary stared at her husband, as if not comprehending what he was saying. "I suppose so."

To his credit, Neil remained undeterred. He felt the need to provide something for his daughter in this exchange. "Absolutely. Her work is just as important as being a soldier."

Mary laughed. Unlike the merry sound that Ruth had grown up with when her mother's fancy was tickled, this laugh had a hard edge to it. "Really, Neil. The girls working while the men are away is fine and all, but certainly not the same work that Frank and the boys are doing. They're risking their lives every day for our freedom."

"Mary!" Neil's voice was as sharp as it ever got. Even Ruth startled. "That's an awful thing to say."

Mary looked at her husband, seeming on the verge of countering him. She shrugged, ultimately deciding she didn't have the energy even for this. "Of course your work is important, dear. We're proud of you, too."

Ruth's eyes stung with tears and no small degree of hurt. She knew what she was doing was valuable to the war effort and she was proud, not only of herself, but of the other women on the line. Willing herself not to cry, she leaned over and kissed her father again. "I better be going. See you tomorrow." She stopped in front of her mother and kissed her cheek without making eye contact.

Walking toward Lillian's house, Ruth tried to shed the pain and hurt of the day. First Cora in the breakroom and now her own mother. It seemed that no one understood her in Evansville. She looked up and saw Lillian sitting on her porch, shelling peas. She was waiting for Ruth. The realization washed away the day's damage and Ruth smiled, thankful to be going home to the one person in Evansville who *did* understand her.

Evansville was land-locked but did offer a beautiful lake, which was the destination of choice on hot summer weekends. Ruth had spent countless afternoons at Lake Kipper, many as a child with her family, many with friends as a teenager, but none were quite like going to the lake with Lillian.

Being at the lake with Lillian, *my lover*, Ruth thought happily, was exciting. She felt emboldened, being with this woman in public. In many ways, it felt like a date. They had held hands walking to the beach, nothing that would attract attention—they might just have been good pals. They sat close together on the blanket, laughing and talking. When Lillian stood up to go into the water, Ruth enjoyed a good long stare at the fair-haired beauty. Lillian was wearing a two-piece bathing suit, part of the war effort to save materials and what Neiman-Marcus had tagged "patriotic chic." Her long legs and full cleavage made Ruth acutely aware of what a genius Neiman-Marcus was. They had brought along Lillian's camera, a wedding present, and took pictures of one another. Only they knew that there was no film in the camera. Playing photographer gave them the opportunity to pose for one another, to tease provocatively, and to focus on one another intimately without anyone giving it a thought.

By the time they settled in for a leisurely nap in the sun, Ruth was fully aroused. It had been liberating to interact with Lillian in such an open way, outside of the confines of their cozy "playing house" world. The thrill of being who she was meant to be was intoxicating. Laying on her stomach, her forearm touching Lillian's, Ruth fought the need to slip a hand underneath and between her own legs. She comforted herself with the thought that when they got home, they would be free to make love with abandon. The image made her sigh aloud.

"You okay?" Lillian asked without opening her eyes. Her voice was drowsy.

"Yes. Just looking forward to tonight."

Lillian peeled one eye open and smiled at Ruth. She discreetly ran a long finger down Ruth's arm. "Me, too."

Ruth tried to think of something else, lest she drive herself mad. She closed her eyes and relaxed, thinking she might doze like Lillian. Her mind remained busy, however. She thought about how happy she was, how complete she felt. The smile was on her face when, once again, she remembered that the country was at war. As had been the case many times since she moved in with Lillian, Ruth sometimes forgot the outside world, her own world having become so full and joyous. The smile fell into a grimace as Ruth wrestled with the familiar guilt. Was it right that she should be so happy, when so many were suffering so mightily? Should she be doing more to help? After all, here she was, enjoying a leisurely afternoon on the beach, planning an evening of passion afterwards, when across the world, life was grim, dark, and infinitely dangerous.

She looked at Lillian, who was now asleep. Her face was at rest in a peaceful pose, with a slight smile at the ends of her lips. Closing her eyes again, Ruth allowed herself to enjoy the moment and push her worries off for another day.

Chapter Six

After church one Sunday, Ruth spent the afternoon with her family. Or at least, what was left of it. With Frank at war and Ruth living with Lillian, the Carroway house was a shell of what it had been. Adding to the emptiness was Mary's increasing level of nervousness. Like all war mothers, she tried to be brave and, of course, was worried for her son, but Mary was close to becoming non-functional. She rarely slept, had lost weight, and looked gaunt and pale.

"I'm worried about her," Neil said to Ruth. The two were in the Carroway victory garden, sent to collect tomatoes. "She's taken this very hard."

Ruth looked up from the tomatoes. She rarely, if ever, heard her stoic father talk like this. "Should we ask Doctor Albert to call on her?"

"No, I don't think there is anything Doctor Albert can do, unless he can bring this war to an end." Neil smiled sadly. "Maybe if you could come around a little more..." Neil was uncomfortable with the request, being unaccustomed to emotional matters, which he left almost exclusively to his wife. Having been in war himself, he held a deep and pervasive fear for his only son's safety but would never admit it to Mary. He knew Frank had a duty to serve and prayed nightly that he would come home in one piece. He was worried, too. Neil had been a bachelor for a long time before meeting Mary. An older father, he had struggled in some ways with showing affection for his children but adored them nonetheless.

"Oh no, I'm sorry, Pop. I guess I should be home more. With the factory work and being at Lillian's, I really haven't been around much."

"Don't blame yourself. You're doing good work at the plant. Real good work."

Ruth was quick to notice that Lillian had been left out of her father's response. "Do you think I should be living at home, not Lillian's?"

"Well, you're doing a kind thing, helping the girl out when her husband is on the front. She must be worried sick, the two of them being newly married. I'm sure she finds your company a comfort."

There was something unspoken and Ruth knew her father was having trouble getting it out. "But you think I should be home."

"I didn't say that."

"But you didn't *not* say that," Ruth pointed out. Her stomach had quickly tied itself in a knot at the mere thought of being away from Lillian, at the thought of returning to her small bed alone at night.

"It's just that some folks think it looks a little disrespectful."

"Disrespectful?"

Neil was now acutely uncomfortable. He focused his gaze squarely on the tomato plant he was working on. "Some folks think you two are too playful, having too much fun together while there is a war going on. Lots of people are suffering and they see you gallivanting all over together, laughing and carrying on at the lake and so on. That's all."

Ruth suspected that wasn't all. She wondered if her father's refusal to make eye contact and the subtext of the "disrespectful" complaints was the same sort of gossip she heard at the factory. The problem was that people were suspicious that she and Lillian were "too close." Blood rushed to Ruth's cheeks. Not only was she mortified to be on the cusp of a discussion with her father about her sexual relationship with a woman, she was also furious that the people of the town were gossiping about and judging her. It was none of their damn business!

But what about her mother? Ruth couldn't bear to see her suffer. "Should I move back in?" Her heart sank as the words left her mouth. She didn't want to be the good daughter. She didn't want to move back in. She wanted to stay right where she was—in Lillian's life and in her bed. She knew Gerald would be coming back at some point and when that happened, she would deal with it the best way that she could. But she couldn't bear to leave a moment before she had to.

Finally, her father looked at her. "I'll take care of your mother. And don't stop coming to Sunday dinner."

≈≈≈≈

Sunday dinners weren't what they used to be, not what they were like before the war. The rationing that was everyone's duty changed the makeup of their dinners—less sugar and oil, more vegetables from the victory garden. But really, what was as it had been before the war?

The Carroway family was finding that America at war was a different America. News from the front was on the forefront of everyone's mind, whether you had a son or husband over there or not. Most, of course, had at least one loved one in harm's way. The Davis family, just down the street from the Carroways, in fact had four men at war. There was Dr. Davis, who, in his forties, was not the typical soldier but had volunteered nonetheless, serving as a doctor in the war effort. And then there were the boys, all three of the Davis sons. They boys had been born in short order, eighteen months apart, and as a result, had provided Uncle Sam with a tidy package of an eighteen-year old, a twenty-year old, and a twenty-one-year old. Dreadfully young, but perfect for the cause. That left Mrs. Davis and her daughter, Melinda, to remain at home, their hours filled with endless worry. The neighbors took good care of the Davis women, inviting them often to dinner, accompanying them to church, and making small talk about everything except the fact that their entire world was in mortal danger every single day.

Mrs. Davis and Melinda had joined the Carroways for a number of Sunday dinners since the war, but they weren't present for this one. Instead, Neil, Mary, and Ruth sat around their table, painfully aware of the seat that was empty, and tried to enjoy the dinner that Mary had prepared. Mary had always enjoyed cooking for her family, but since Frank's absence, cooking had become a chore and Mary nearly an automaton.

"Delicious dinner, dear," Neil said, smiling at his wife. He worried about her and thought the constant stress of worrying about their eldest child was tearing her apart inside.

"Thank you," Mary said, dipping her head modestly.

Ruth was in a bad mood. Being in the house reminded her of her "old life." Her life before Lillian. Sitting at the same table at which she had sat as a child and an adolescent and a young adult made her acutely aware of the changes in her life. She liked her new life and was itching to finish the dinner. The place setting that Mary insisted on putting out at every meal was a stark reminder of Frank, as if any of them needed one. Ruth knew she shouldn't say anything, but found the words coming out of her mouth anyway.

"Why do you set Frank's place every night, Mom? It's morbid."

Mary's eyes flashed, a rare emotion outside of the omnipresent solemnity that she had been carrying since Frank left. "Why wouldn't I?"

Ruth could tell right away that she should have listened to her instinct and not said anything, but it was too late for that. "Well, he's obviously not here. Why take the time to put out his plate and then put it back away at every meal?"

Mary put her fork down deliberately. "What if you were over there, Ruth? Would you want your family to forget you? To enjoy these meals in safety and comfort while you suffered across the ocean, cold, hungry, and afraid?" Her voice was strident but the pain in her heart seeped through.

"No, of course not. I didn't mean any disrespect," Ruth backtracked.

"Of course you didn't, Ruth. Let's just enjoy this meal and be thankful for what we have." Neil was always the calming influence. Even with Neil's calm, however, the tone of the evening had been tainted and the family hurried through the rest of their meal with very little conversation.

Ruth made the short walk to Lillian's house after dinner. As she walked, she realized that she thought of it is as walking "home." Was that what she was doing? Making a home with Lillian? Did Lillian feel the same way? If that wasn't what was happening, what was? The questions made Ruth feel unsettled.

Shaking her head to clear her mind as she entered the front door, unlocked as always, she told herself to be thankful for what she had. Who would have ever dreamed that she would be sleeping with a woman, experiencing the physical feelings that she had with Lillian? Certainly not Ruth. She felt the now familiar flip in her stomach when she heard Lillian call out for her.

"Ruthie? Is that you? I'm in here."

It was nice, Ruth thought. Being missed, being wanted. She had never imagined it could feel like this. She walked into the bedroom, smiling instantly when she saw Lillian stretched out on the bed in her pajamas, reading a book. She had read the book before, *The Heart is a Lonely Hunter*, but she didn't want to spend extra money on new ones.

"You look comfortable," Ruth said as she sat on the edge of the bed.

"I am. More now, I think." Lillian put her hand lightly on Ruth's, causing a thrill of intimacy in both of them. "How was dinner?"

"Fine. Sort of. Mom is just so sad about Frank. It's like a funeral every time I go over there. Plus I made her angry asking about Frank's place setting at the table for every dinner."

Lillian frowned. She knew Ruth had a somewhat different perspective on the war. Her brother was over there, but not her husband. But then, did Lillian have a right to lay claim to a special level of distress, considering what she had been doing with Ruth? It was something that had crossed her mind more than once. But for now, the experiences that she was sharing with Ruth were too powerful for her to dig deeply into questions like that. Still, a nagging sense of guilt and betrayal was always the unwelcome aftermath of their time together. Lillian wondered if that would fade at some point, or if it should. She gestured to the nightstand. "I got letters from Gerald today. Two of them."

Ruth looked at the little stack of correspondence, noting that it was written in pencil with what appeared to be a clumsy hand. She felt immediate resentment. She knew that Lillian was married, but even so, every time Gerald came up it made her feel uncomfortable. "Oh? How is he?" She tried to force her voice to sound genuine. But her tone did not match her feelings. She didn't want Gerald to suffer harm; she wasn't a monster. But she didn't want Lillian to think about him often, if at all. It was unrealistic, she realized, but this was the first time she had ever been in love with a woman. It was difficult navigating the new terrain.

"He didn't say much about how things are over there. Mostly asked about me and things here in town." Lillian ran her finger over the bedspread, avoiding eye contact. "And he said he missed me desperately."

Despite her efforts, Ruth couldn't stop herself from frowning. Gerald was sure to miss Lillian, desperately even. Why wouldn't he? Around the world in wartime, with his beautiful wife here at home, alone? He'd be crazy not to miss her. *But she's mine now*, Ruth found herself thinking. But was she? "I'm sure he does." It was all she could manage.

Lillian continued drawing patterns on the bedspread. "Do you mind it very much when I talk about him?" She already knew the answer. For all of her charms, Lillian could be manipulative. Within her confusion about what she was doing was a sense of power. She knew that Ruth was in love with her, just as Gerald was. It felt good to be desired, a welcome escape from the drudgery of wartime Indiana.

Ruth waited before answering. She decided to be honest. "Yes."

The word hung heavy between them. Lillian broke the silence after several long moments.

"He's my husband, after all. It's only natural that he would miss me."

Ruth flushed with emotion and turned to Lillian. "But do you miss him? I'm not your husband; I know that. But what we have, what we've been doing. What does it mean to you?" She didn't stop for an answer, afraid to hear it before she got her feelings out. "Because it means everything to me. I love you, Lil."

Tears welled in Lillian's eyes, involuntarily. It was at that moment that she made a momentous realization. She loved this woman. She loved her in a different, deeper, more intimate way than she loved Gerald. The heights of their physical passion, the contentment of their connection, it was all so different than with Gerald. "And I love you, Ruth Carroway."

Ruth's eyes widened. She knew she had been taking a chance by revealing her feelings to Lillian, but nothing could have stopped her in that moment. Overcome by emotion, she pulled her lover to her, holding her close. She reveled in the feel of their bodies pressing together and let Lillian's words echo in her mind. *And I love you.* Words escaped her, but actions didn't.

The touch of their lips was becoming familiar, but not so much so that every kiss wasn't a delightful new experience. When Lillian parted her lips slightly, Ruth pushed into Lillian's mouth. The warmth of their tongues when they touched felt electric and urged each of them to kiss with a delicious intensity.

After, Lillian pulled a package of cigarettes from her nightstand drawer. She knew Ruth didn't like her smoking, but sometimes, she needed the comfort of a cigarette. She nestled her head in the crook of Ruth's bent arm, enjoying the lingering scent of their lovemaking, the scent of Ruth.

"This is nice, isn't it?" Ruth asked.

Blowing a small cone of smoke upwards, Lillian responded. "Yes. Very."

"It's like we've escaped the real world."

They lay quietly for long minutes, the time relished by both. Lillian finished her cigarette and stubbed it out in a heavy glass ashtray. Her hands now free, she touched Ruth's stomach, caressing her lightly.

"I don't want this to end, Lil." Ruth's words caused her to inhale immediately after they were spoken. She was nervous.

Lillian stopped caressing for a moment and then resumed before answering. "I don't either, sweetheart."

Ruth's heart filled with happiness, just as it did every time that Lillian used a term of endearment toward her. It made Ruth feel as if their relationship was real, more than just sex. "But what will happen… when he comes back?" Ruth tensed. She knew this was dangerous ground. As much as she wanted the answer, she was terrified it might not be the one she was hoping for.

Lillian sighed. It was a long, melancholy sigh, one intimating that Lil did not desire this conversation. "Ruth, I honestly don't know what will happen when he comes home. Can't we just enjoy what we have now?"

Ruth fidgeted as she fought warring impulses to let it drop and push forward. But Ruth was Ruth and she'd never been known for a tendency to hesitate. "I adore what we have now; you know I do. But I need to know what happens next." There, she'd said it.

Another long sigh. "Please don't push me on this. I just don't want to think about that right now."

"But don't you think Gerald would want you to be happy? Happy like you are now, with me?" Even as she said it, Ruth knew her words were ridiculous. No, Gerald would most certainly not want his wife to be happy. Not if it meant surrendering her to "one of those kinds of girls"...to a girl like Ruth. Why had she said it? Was she spoiling for a fight?

Whatever Ruth's motivation, Lillian didn't take the bait. She continued caressing Ruth's smooth skin. Making love with Ruth was her escape, a perfect way to ignore the war, the world, and Lillian's own internal struggle with her sexuality. For her, and for now, it was enough. But she knew these words would hurt her paramour. Ruth had never been married and Lillian believed that it was therefore impossible to understand the particular struggle that Lillian was battling. So, Lillian said nothing and returned to the language that they both understood. She dipped her hand lower and kissed Ruth's neck.

Ruth knew she was being put off. But for the moment, with Lillian's warm, soft body pressing into hers and with the growing need resurging in her center, Ruth allowed it.

Chapter Seven

That Saturday morning was bright and sunny. Lillian and Ruth lingered in bed, far longer than usual, enjoying the respite from their early morning wake-ups.

"We should get up and do the wash. Get it on the line to dry," Lillian said, her bare arms wrapped around Ruth.

Ruth kissed Lillian's shoulder. "I have a better idea." She moved a hand under the sheet, still rumpled from the previous night's pleasures.

"Ruth Carroway! You always have a better idea." Lillian laughed.

"I don't hear you complaining."

"How could I? What we do...it feels so amazing. I'm embarrassed to say I feel like I can't get enough." Lillian looked sheepishly at Ruth to see her reaction.

"That's perfect, Lil. I feel that way, too."

Ruth found Lillian's wetness under the sheet. She entered her and groaned when she felt Lillian spread her legs wide to welcome Ruth. No one had ever taught Ruth what to do. No one had to. Instinctively, she entered Lillian again and again, touching her in the right spot, while Lillian moaned and cried out in pleasure. Just as Lillian's climax approached, a loud rap at the front door interrupted the sounds of their lovemaking.

In the throes of passion and beside herself with

desire, Lillian begged Ruth to keep going. "Please, Ruth. Don't stop now."

Distracted by the intrusion, Ruth found her rhythm again and soon returned Lillian to edge of her peak. With a final few movements against her pubis, Ruth took Lillian the rest of the way, with Lillian crying out Ruth's name just as the rap at the door sounded again.

Gently, Ruth removed herself and hurried to the front room, leaving Lillian spent on the bed. She could see through the living room window a dark, official-looking car parked in front of the house. The smile on her face from hearing Lillian call her name at the moment of her greatest ecstasy died. She knew what that car meant. It was the sight every family member and loved one feared during wartime. That car had been on the street before and it never brought good news.

"Lillian, you need to get dressed as quickly as you can. There is someone here for you."

※ ※ ※ ※

The next morning, Ruth awoke early only to find Lillian already awake and lying beside her. Lillian's eyes were swollen nearly shut from crying and lack of sleep. Ruth felt instantly protective of her and a deep swell of love swept over her. She moved closer to her and wrapped an arm around her, only to have Lillian push it away.

"Don't." Lillian's voice was cold and flat.

"What? Why?"

"I need you to get out of my bed."

Ruth was now fully awake. "What are you talking

about?"

Lying on her back and staring straight up, Lillian addressed the ceiling. "You know why Gerald got killed? Because I'm being punished. Punished for what I've done with you."

"Lillian, you can't possibly believe that—"

"I can and I do. Not only did I betray my husband, I did it with a woman." Lillian's voice broke and she paused. When she resumed speaking, there was no emotion. "I'll never forget that when that chaplain was walking up my steps to tell me that my husband had been blown apart, fighting for his country, I was in my husband's bed, letting a woman put her fingers inside of me. I'll never forgive myself. Or you."

☙☙❧❧

Lillian's mother was a formidable woman. Margaret Howell was a no-nonsense type and when there was a job to be done, by God, she got it done. The job to be done at the moment was that of mourning her son-in-law and comforting her young, newly widowed daughter. Ruth simply did not fit into the picture.

The instant Margaret arrived, the small house, which had felt so cozy and warm when it had just been Lillian and Ruth, became cramped and cold. Ruth felt very much the outsider and Margaret went to no trouble to make her feel any differently.

When Ruth came home from the factory on the second day of Margaret's stay, she found Margaret busy in a flurry of activity. Sheets were being changed, the floors had been mopped, and there seemed to be constant motion. In stark contrast, Lillian sat like a statue on the couch, smoking cigarette after cigarette and staring at nothing. It looked like she hadn't showered since the moment of the dreadful announcement. Standing in the entryway, Ruth stared at the woman who she had professed her love to just days ago. Things were so different now; it seemed like a lifetime ago.

"Lil?" Ruth said softly, trying not only to startle her but also to avoid Margaret's attention. It seemed that anytime Ruth tried to talk to Lillian, Margaret was immediately in the room to intervene. She had also taken over sleeping beside her daughter "to comfort her poor girl," as she had said. Ruth could hardly argue otherwise and Lillian certainly did not put up a fight.

Lillian looked over and stared at Ruth with dead eyes. She didn't speak and instead took another long drag on her cigarette. Gone were the warm sparkle and the electric sexuality between the two of them.

"Are you okay? Can I get you anything?"

Before Lillian could answer, if she had any inclination to answer, Margaret swept into the room. Ruth wondered if she had been keeping watch.

"She's not up to talking, Ruth."

The women engaged in a brief stare-down, neither giving an inch. Margaret's eyes held such disdain and reproach for Ruth that Ruth was sure she must have figured out what had been going on between her and her daughter. The next moment made the suspicion clear.

"I've packed your things," Margaret said with an almost satisfied tone.

Ruth blinked. "What?" It was all she could think to say.

"I said I've packed your things."

Ruth looked at Lillian, who continued to stare

off. "But, I've been staying here with Lillian."

Lillian blew out a long stream of cigarette smoke, drawing the attention of both her mother and her former lover. Any thoughts or emotions she might have had floated away in the wisps of smoke, unheard.

Ruth felt a panic rise within her. *This can't be happening*, she thought. "Lil? Please say something, Lil."

Margaret crossed her arms and tapped her toe. "Lillian doesn't want you to stay any longer, Ruth. Your being here is upsetting her; can't you see that?"

Lillian didn't seem upset. Lillian didn't seem anything at all. In fact, Lillian did not seem to be aware of the scene taking place around her, despite being the central figure of the conversation. She stubbed her cigarette out, rose from the couch, stretched her long limbs as if she had just rose from a relaxing nap, and left the room without a word.

Even Margaret seemed surprised by the exit, although she certainly would never admit that to the young woman who she suspected of having inappropriate "relations" with her daughter. "I hope you're happy now," she snapped. "It's not enough she's lost her husband, now you have to make a scene. Why can't you do the right thing and just go?"

Ruth ignored the ugly words and followed Lillian into the bedroom, where she found Lillian sitting on the bed. She tried to ignore the memories seeing the bed immediately brought to mind.

"Lil?"

Here, at least, Lillian granted Ruth the courtesy of looking in her direction when spoken to. Ruth was startled at the utter lack of emotion in the blue eyes that had once held such affection for her. She swallowed hard against the lump in the throat.

"Your mother is throwing me out of your house."

"So I gather."

"Did you tell her to do it?"

"I didn't tell her not to do it," Lillian said, looking back toward the wall rather than Ruth.

"I don't understand. Why are you doing this?" Ruth felt the tears now, warm and full. She knelt on the hard floor near Lillian. "Why?"

The new widow glanced down at Ruth, who had cast herself as a desperate and vulnerable figure, literally at Lillian's feet. A whisper of passion remembered wound its way through her body. Closing her eyes against the unbidden feeling, Lillian found the cold, empty part inside of herself that she had been clinging to since the chaplain knocked at the door. The part that she told herself she deserved and would always deserve for what she had done, no matter what she might feel. "What happened between us was just a lark. It was silly and wrong. I don't want you here to remind me of my mistake. It's as simple as that."

A slight tremble in Lillian's final words threatened to betray her cold exterior but Ruth was so devastated and emotional that she missed the nuance. Her hurt evanesced into anger, a defense mechanism more than anything, and she struck back.

"You're a coward, you know that?" Ruth stood up so that she could look Lillian in the face. "I know you don't believe what you're saying. I know I made you feel things in bed that Gerald never did. Maybe God will punish me for speaking ill of the dead, but it's the truth. You're just like me, Lillian Reed. Only you're afraid to be happy." Ruth's eyes flashed with anger as she waited for a reaction.

Lillian's face flushed red. This was all too confusing and hard. It would be easier just to forget.

❧❧❧❧

Gerald's body remained in Europe, where he had died. Like most soldiers who lost their lives, Gerald had been buried in a temporary national cemetery overseas, his remains alongside his many comrades in arms, each too young. A funeral was held in Evansville and although she knew she likely wasn't welcome, Ruth felt compelled to be there. Once she was there, she wished fervently to be anywhere but.

Gerald Reed had been an only son and his loss was etched on the face of his stricken parents as well as two younger sisters. Ruth listened as a clergyman spoke warmly of Gerald, a man he had never met. The pastor did a fine job of narrating the accomplishments of Gerald's short life, his high school sports achievements, his marriage to young Lillian, and then, of course, his heroics with the 654th Tank Destroyer Battalion. Ruth suspected that the pastor had given similar remarks so many times that it was near rote. To his credit, he managed to convey the sense that he had known the fallen hero. When he got to the part about Gerald giving his life for his country, his mother wailed, no longer able to keep her grief inside.

Ruth sat respectfully in the back of the room. She didn't have a connection with Gerald, other than Lillian, of course. And one did not make that kind of small talk with other mourners. Ruth grimaced at Gerald's mother's keening, feeling badly for her and also feeling badly for imagining her own mother in a similar situation. Thank God, Frank was safe and that his letters had been coming through regularly. She stole a glance at Lillian, who was sitting in the front row in a black dress. From her angle, Ruth could only see the side of her face and it revealed nothing.

Lillian looked like a statue, beautiful but emotionless. Ruth wished she knew what her former lover was thinking. But Lillian gave no clues and didn't offer Ruth even a glance. Ruth was as dead to her as Gerald, who was buried and would remain forever oblivious of his wife's transgression as he lay in a simple grave in Colleville-sur-Mer, France.

The attendees had all suffered a loss. For most of them, it was the promise of their young son, husband, brother, and friend. For Ruth, it was the seemingly ephemeral moments of happiness with Lillian.

Chapter Eight

The first weeks after Gerald's funeral dragged for Ruth. She slogged her way through each day at the factory, with nothing to look forward to after her shift. She no longer had Lillian to go home to, no longer had Lillian to hold, no longer had Lillian to make love to. At home, things felt different. Ruth was hyper aware of the reversal of her fortunes. Now, she was just the youngest child, back at her parents' home, with its pall of dread as her mother waited for news, any news, of Frank. Ruth felt alone, at home and at work. She had no place here, she realized.

Lying in bed, trying to sleep, Ruth had a realization. If she didn't have a place here in this small town, with its small-minded people and its small spot on the map, why not leave? Frank wasn't the only one who could make a difference. Women were being welcomed into the Red Cross Nurse Corps, even those without prior training. Maybe helping the cause would take her mind off of her broken heart, Ruth thought. Even if it didn't, at least she would be making a difference. She imagined herself overseas, in an exciting new country, working hard and meeting new people. *It would be a whole new life*, Ruth thought. *Exactly what I need.* A plan formed and hope restored, Ruth fell into a deep sleep, the best she had had since her last night with Lillian.

"How could you do this to me?"

Ruth blinked at her mother's desperate question. As she had expected, her mother had not welcomed the news that she planned to volunteer to help with the war overseas.

Despite where she was heading, somewhere where she would have to grow up in an instant, Ruth felt like a little girl, crushed at having disappointed her mother.

"I want to help, that's all."

"Help? You can help here at home, like I do. You don't need to go over there. You're just a girl. It's too dangerous."

Mary looked to her husband for support. "Say something, Neil. Tell her she can't go." Mary twisted the dishtowel she had been using when Ruth blurted out the news. Her knuckles were white and as Ruth watched her, her mother's hands suddenly looked very old.

"We can't tell her what to do, dear. She's a grown woman. It's her choice." Neil spoke softly and hated the words as he said them but knew they were true. His own heart was torn. He was proud of his daughter, seeking out a duty that she could easily have avoided without judgment. But he was also afraid, as any father would be. Added to the fear for his children was a fear that if anything happened to either of them, his wife would be shattered, beyond his reach to repair.

"I'll be in my room," Ruth said. Nobody stopped her.

Is there a way for a young woman to prepare to go to war? Ruth alternated between excitement and fear on a daily, almost hourly, basis. One thing that had provided some comfort was the structure of her packing list. Provided by a helpful senior nurse from the Nurse Corps, Ruth had been proud of receiving the official correspondence, tangible proof that she, Ruth Carroway, was going overseas to serve her country.

The list, typewritten and numbered, with chatty helpful hints interspersed, contained reminders that the trip wasn't a lark, not by any means.

Shoes, take extra as these are rationed overseas.
Nail polish, but colors brighter than Windsor are taboo in some theatres.
We will meet you at the port; remember security! Do not say "good-bye" as that will invite questions.

Ruth's eyes had widened at the reminders and realized that she had needed a nudge, telling her that this wasn't just a way to escape heartbreak. She was going into an active war zone. *No wonder Mother is worried,* she thought as she re-folded a stack of underwear and tucked the stack in her large trunk. The few remaining items to be packed were strewn across her bedroom floor and Ruth frowned at them, wondering how she would get everything to fit. Nursing uniforms, a nursing cap with a set of pins that she did not yet know how to use, a cape, bedding. There was so much to remember. *Don't count on adding to your gear in the theatre—pack smartly!* the list had admonished.

A knock at the door interrupted the packing. Ruth looked up and saw her mother. She immediately braced herself. Mother would now be making her last, emotional plea, begging her daughter not to go. But that was not why Mary was there.

"Honey, Lillian is here to see you," Mary said. She stood in the doorway and her eyes took in the gear being packed. It was too much for her, too much like the scene far too recently when she had watched her firstborn excitedly pack his Army gear.

Lillian stepped in and dipped her head politely at Mary. "Thank you, Mrs. Carroway."

Emotion had stolen Mary's voice and she could only nod in response before leaving.

Lillian repeated what Mary had just done and looked at all of the packing activity going on in Ruth's small bedroom. For a moment, her heart wavered. She had loved this woman, after all, at least she thought she had. And now, now she was leaving. Lillian tightened her jaw, forcing herself to be strong.

Ruth watched the warring impulses travel over her former lover's face, just as similar impulses raced through her own body. Lillian had not had a kind word for her since that awful day and the sudden and total shift in their relationship had scarred Ruth.

The women stood in silence, staring at one another. Finally, her emotions contained, Lillian spoke.

"So, you're going to war?"

"That's right."

"Why?" Lillian carefully kept a sharp edge to her voice. It was easier to forget the closeness she had shared with Ruth if she sounded angry. At least, that was what Lillian was banking on.

"Well, there's not much for me here, is there? Besides, I want to help."

"You, Gerald, all of the boys who don't come back. You all feel so brave, so self-righteous, don't you?

Running off to war to help the cause. What about the ones that are left behind? The war made me a widow, you know." A tremor of emotion entered Lillian's voice.

Ruth's heart leapt. Was Lillian asking her to stay? Was she likening her to her own husband? Worrying that she would once again lose her love? She looked finally at Lillian.

Lillian's hard, defiant gaze rested on Ruth. She raised her chin a bit, daring Ruth to challenge her.

There was no energy in Ruth for this fight. Lillian had made her feelings clear when she kicked her out of her home.

"I can't speak to that, Lillian. All I can say is that I can't stay here any longer and I want to help our boys." Ruth's voice said far more than her words.

The women held each other's gaze, neither speaking. It was a battle of the wills. Finally, Lillian shrugged and turned to leave. "Well, good luck to you." She began to walk out, then stopped. "And I know you took that page from Gerald's girlie magazine."

※ ※ ※ ※

Ruth checked her trunk for the fourth time. Feeling unsettled, she sat on her childhood bed and looked around her room. *Maybe for the last time ever*, she thought to herself. The comfort and security that the room had once represented had become stifling, the twin bed a mocking reminder of her shared bed with Lillian and all of the delight it had brought. No, she no longer belonged here.

Her heart ached for her former lover and with it, a new feeling. The feeling that something inside of her had been revealed and unleashed—something that

Ruth knew she could no longer ignore. The physical pleasure that she had experienced making love with Lillian made her hungry for more. It was more than that, though, Ruth knew. She also longed for the emotional connection that had been forming with Lillian. The hint of what it could be was damningly tortuous. Ruth suspected there was more of it out there for her—but where?

Not for the first time, she wondered what would be happening if there was no war. Would she have had the courage to leave if there weren't a place for her to go?

A knock at her doorframe saved her from answering her own question. Ruth looked up to see her father standing in the threshold.

"Pop. How long have you been there?"

Neil smiled and stepped inside of his only daughter's room. "Long enough to know you've got a lot on that mind of yours. Only natural, I suppose. Today's the day, huh?" Neil's casual words belied the fear he felt. Having seen war up close, he wanted nothing more than to spare his youngest child from the things that he knew she would see.

"Today's the day. Mom still mad?"

Mary had made no effort to conceal her anger about Ruth's decision to leave Indiana, "by choice!" as she had emphasized to her husband. Already overwrought with constant worry and dread about her son being on the front, the notion of her daughter voluntarily putting herself in harm's way had driven her to a resentful ire that made the last week of Ruth's time at home tense and uncomfortable for everyone. Underlying the anger, of course, was a mother's worst fear, the possible loss of not only one but now both of her beloved children. The fact that Ruth had volunteered for the duty only increased Mary's emotions. Caught between warring emotions of maternal pride over her daughter's bravery and a soul-deep terror of losing her as a result, the terror won out.

"You know she's only worried about you. She's sick about you leaving."

Ruth toyed with the handle of her suitcase to avoid looking in her father's eyes. She knew that her mother wasn't the only one dreading her crossing the Atlantic. She also knew that her father was trying to spare her the guilt of leaving.

"I know. I feel awful about making her upset." Ruth was telling the truth. She had lain in bed night after night thinking about the pain that she was inflicting on her mother by volunteering for the war. Adding to the internal conflict was the fact that Ruth's reason for leaving had just as much to do with helping the cause as it did removing herself from Lillian's orbit, which had become too painful.

"It's something you have to do, I understand." Despite his non-emotional exterior, Neil did understand. He sensed that his daughter was at a crossroads in her life. The fact that it intersected with the nation being at war was an unfortunate happenstance. "I'll take care of the home front, okay?"

With that, Ruth did meet her father's eyes. In them, she saw compassion and acceptance. She wouldn't dream of confiding in him about Lillian or about the feelings she was experiencing towards women. But her heart eased a bit when she realized that her father was on her side and that even though he surely did not want both of his children at risk any more than his wife did, he knew that Ruth would not find what she needed in Evansville.

    A wave of emotion overtook Ruth and she threw her arms around Neil. The stoic veteran of his own war embraced her, closing his eyes in silent prayer that she would be safe.

Chapter Nine

Ruth's first sight of Europe was anti-climactic. The six weeks of training provided by the Red Cross center in Staten Island had been a blur of information, studying, and meeting other young women like her—each young, nervous, but excited about joining the war effort. Not a single one of them had ever been overseas and most had never been out of their home state. Ruth had absorbed the training, focusing her mind completely on the many procedures and tasks that she would soon be responsible for. It had been a welcome distraction and there were several days during which she realized she had not thought about Lillian at all.

The training was intense but interesting. Ruth found herself learning about ward duty one day and sanitation procedures the next. She learned to administer injections, take vital signs, and read medical charts. She excelled during the basic anatomy course and took quickly to the instruction on medicines. Many of the women had blanched when shown the film on wartime injuries. The short movie spared no detail in showing close-up injuries of men wounded in battle. The grim narration told the young nurses that they would see all of this and much more in wartime and emphasized the injuries that they were likely to see most often. Ruth took careful notes to detail what she was learning about shrapnel wounds, amputations, dysentery, and the like. It hadn't been long since Ruth last sat in a high school classroom, but these classes were certainly nothing like those days.

Ruth had been recognized as particularly adept during training and told she was confirmed for a position overseas, rather than on the home front. It had taken no time at all for Ruth to agree. She would go wherever the country needed her and if that was overseas, that was where she wanted to go. She was given her assignment: London. It sounded very exciting and exotic to Ruth.

After the brief graduation ceremony, the women had made their rushed good-byes, hugs, and promises to stay in touch, fueled by the ever-present urgency that wartime brought with it. Ruth and the others had been issued their nurse's uniforms and were assigned to ships immediately to go overseas where they were needed. Most of the other nurses onboard were military nurses, looking sharp in their uniforms with their rank insignia. There was no hierarchy, however; each woman was proud of her role and they held one another in high regard, sisters at arms.

Ruth learned quite quickly that sea life was not for her. The first day on the ship, she made the mistake of eating far too much. It was only later that she realized the mess hall had been empty because the others had been warned that what went in would inevitably come up. The rest of the trip saw Ruth essentially confined to her small bunk room, which she shared with a kind and patient woman from Virginia, Lettie. Lettie had been a saint, bringing Ruth small meals of soup and dry crackers and not getting upset even when Ruth was up multiple times during the nights to rush to the head.

So, when the hospital ship arrived and the

women were prepared to disembark, her first sight of another country failed to move Ruth. All she cared about was stepping on dry land, which was blessedly stationary and didn't rock and heave side to side. With tearful good-byes to friends made during the journey, the women separated, heading out with their assigned units and preparing to enter a new phase of their lives.

≫≫≪≪

After checking in at the hospital in London where she was assigned, Ruth made her way to the bunkroom. The head nurse had told her that she could pick any open bunk she liked and that her duty would start first thing in the morning. After that, she sent Ruth on her way with a perfunctory "good luck." Ruth was realizing quickly that there was no time for handholding on the front.

Upon entering the bunkroom, Ruth was pleased to see that it had the familiar look of the dormitory she had stayed at during training. There were two dozen bunks, twelve on each side of the room, each with a small table on the side. Many bunks were obviously spoken for, as was evident by the linens on the bed and footlockers arranged in front. Others lay bare, their mattresses uncovered.

Ruth spotted an open bunk in the corner of the room. Realizing she was picking her home for the foreseeable future, she decided it looked just as good as any place. She sat down heavily on the bed and exhaled. *I'm really here*, she thought to herself. The travel had been so arduous that in some respects, she had forgotten what was coming, but now, here she was. Ruth Carroway, a trained nurse, assigned to overseas duty in London. She couldn't help but smile. It felt good to be somewhere useful. Even though she had no idea where her brother was, being in London made her feel linked to him, as if they were fellow soldiers fighting a common threat.

Looking around, Ruth noticed the shape of a woman under a sheet in the bunk next to her. She was facing the wall so Ruth couldn't make out her face, but she could see a mound of curly brown hair spilling across the pillow. Sleeping nurses similarly occupied other beds, but one woman was awake and made her way over.

"Welcome. You must be the new girl," she said in a strong New York accent. "I'm Midgie." She extended a hand.

Ruth stood up and shook the woman's hand. "Ruth. Ruth Carroway. Nice to meet you."

"You, too. Let me help you get your linens so you can get your bed set up."

Ruth smiled gratefully and followed her new friend to a hallway where she pulled an armload of sheets and blankets from a mountainous stack. "Thank you so much, Midgie."

"No problem. I've been here seven months but I still remember my first day. It can be overwhelming. Look, hon, I have a shift and have to go but I'll catch up with you later and show you around. Sound good?"

Ruth took the stack from Midgie. "Perfect. Thanks again."

Midgie gave a quick wave as she left and Ruth admired her sharp Army uniform. She was impressed with the confidence and attitude of the woman and hoped, not for the first time, that she could pass the muster.

Thirty minutes later, Ruth had her bed made, her footlocker in place, and some personal items stowed in the small bedside table. She was tired but couldn't sleep. The other women in the room were still asleep and Ruth felt edgy. Struck by inspiration, she decided to give herself a self-tour of the hospital. After all, she would be spending her days there, why not get a quick peek? Dressing quickly in her spotless Red Cross uniform, she set out in search of the hospital.

≪≪≫≫

From behind the door marked "OPERATING ROOM," Ruth could hear a low rumble of chatter and instruments being handed over, placed on metal, and instructions being barked. She knew she shouldn't let herself in, but her curiosity got the better of her. She pulled a cotton mask from a box near the door and placed it on her face. Taking a breath, she pushed open the heavy double doors and walked inside.

The smell of the OR was overwhelming. It hit Ruth all at once and her mind quickly identified the odors. The academic exercise was a welcome diversion from processing everything that was happening in front of her. Antiseptic, strong and sterile. Body odor. Not only did the patients smell, but so did the doctors and nurses. The endless stream of patients and stressful conditions all contributed to a less than hygienic situation. The staff likely didn't even notice that they stank to high heaven. Ruth could not immediately place another smell. It was metallic-smelling, almost like copper. She inhaled sharply, so much so that her facemask pulled in to her nostrils. What was that smell?

"Clamp!" a doctor yelled.

Just as Ruth turned in the direction of the doctor's voice, she saw a spurt of bright red blood rise from the draped figure on the operating table in front of the doctor. She stared at it, thinking of swimming with Frank and how they had squirted water from the lake between their hands to make a fountain. Her mind struggled to process what she was seeing. *That can't be blood*, she thought. *There's too much of it. Whoever's under there couldn't live without all of that blood.*

"God damn it! I said clamp!" the doctor raged.

The nurse at the table snapped a clamp in the doctor's hand and a second later, the fountain subsided.

Ruth continued to stare. The doctor had blood all over his operating smock. There was blood all over the floor. She suddenly felt woozy.

A pair of hands was on her elbows from behind. "Easy there, hon," a pleasant female voice said in her ear. The hands steadied her. "You don't want to pass out. The docs will never let you hear the end of it."

Ruth nodded mutely and allowed herself to be led to another part of the operating room.

"You must be the new nurse," the woman said. "I'm Betty Brower, head nurse here." Betty was a sturdy woman and looked to be in her late thirties. She looked exhausted but even so, her eyes were kind.

Ruth nodded, forcing herself to focus on the woman and not the bloody scene behind her.

"Thank you. I'm sorry; I'm okay now. I just thought..."

Betty smiled. "I know. Just thought you'd see what you were getting into. Well, hon, now you know. There's really no easy way to get the first look. It's not pretty, that's for sure."

Ruth could only nod.

"I have you on the schedule for orientation and your first shift tomorrow morning. Why don't you head back to the bunkroom and get some rest? You're going to need it." With that, Betty shooed Ruth away.

Ruth realized as she walked out of the room what the metallic small had been. It was the smell of human blood. She shivered. *I wonder if I'll ever get used to that?*

※※※※

As it turned out, after the first week, Ruth did learn to get used to the smell of human blood. It no longer registered with her. She hadn't decided if that was a good thing or a bad thing. What she hadn't yet gotten used to was the operating room. Ruth felt clumsy in the OR. The pace was so fast and everyone seemed to know so much more than she did. She knew her brief training in Staten Island couldn't possibly have prepared her for everything she would face, but felt woefully unprepared nonetheless.

Work in the ward was less stressful. Here, the patients were recovering and the pace was manageable. Ruth found that she liked interacting with the patients, but still, an uneasiness gripped her.

Ruth had arrived early for her shift in the ward and was surprised to glance at the clock and see that seven hours had passed. Time had flown by. Betty, supervising the ward, caught Ruth's eye and motioned her over to the small desk where she kept her files.

"A week in, Ruth. How are you doing?" Betty asked.

Ruth hesitated but Betty's eyes, always kind, made her decision for her. She had a feeling Betty would understand. "I'm worried I will make a mistake and maybe hurt one of the patients. Maybe even kill them." Even though the last was said in a whisper, Ruth felt better having gotten her secret fear out.

Betty laughed. "Honey, don't worry about that. You're doing more good here than you can imagine. When things are this bad, it's hard to make them worse."

"That's not very reassuring," Ruth said.

Betty looked over Ruth's shoulder at a new patient, being brought in on gurney. "No time for that now. We've got work to do." With a pat on Ruth's shoulder, Betty was checking on the new arrival.

An hour later, Ruth was just about to finish her shift when a patient called out to her. She did an about-face and stood by his bedside. "Yes? Anything I can do for you?"

"Am I going to be okay, nurse?" the young man asked. Private William Adams was the boy's name and really, he was more boy than man. He couldn't have been more than nineteen. His face, pale from trauma, nonetheless held a boyish charm, even more so because of the sprinkling of freckles across his nose. Ruth stared at him, his shattered body, his lips wrinkled with dehydration, and his eyes that had just a tiny bit of life left in them. She stammered an answer that she knew was inadequate the moment it left her lips.

"Oh, I'm sure you'll be quite fine, soldier. You've got some serious injuries but I bet you'll be just fine." She trailed off as her words made their way to the soldier's consciousness. A flicker of despair passed over his green eyes. Surprisingly, he smiled.

"I was just wondering, that's all." His eyes closed again and did not open them, not even when he made a terrible final gasping sound and not after he fell silent.

Ruth took the man's hand. "Private?" There was no pulse. Hot tears sprang to her eyes and she felt as if she were going to throw up. "Oh God," she whispered. She began to sob.

An instant later, she felt a sharp squeeze at her collarbone. It was Betty.

"Come with me, Carroway."

Outside of the ward, Betty held Ruth by both shoulders. She spoke firmly but without anger. Her eyes were still kind but intense. "You can't cry in front of the boys, do you hear me? Not ever. We must do our crying in private. Do you understand?"

Ruth shook her head mutely, tears still streaming down her face. She wasn't in Indiana anymore.

Chapter Ten

Dear Frank,

Well, brother, you may have already heard from Mother and Pop, but I'm over here with you! I've volunteered with the Red Cross Nursing Corps and am now in London. I know you're not allowed to say where you are but I like to pretend you're somewhere close.

I don't know how long it will take to get this letter but I wanted to catch you up on what your little sis has been doing. Earlier this week we had to participate in gas mask drills. The masks had an awful rubber smell to them but I think that must be preferable to the alternative if we would ever have to use them for real. You'll be proud to know that I tied a nurse named Shorty for the fastest time to "don and doff." We also have had a number of air raid drills. Lots of training all of the time and always the patients to help as well.

I could never have imagined doing these things, but here I am! Just like you must say to yourself every day, I suppose.

I'll say good-bye now and I hope I **don't** see you. I don't want to see you come through my hospital! Be safe and write if you can.

Love,
Ruth

⁂

"I'll never get these pin clips to work," Ruth muttered. With all of the new things that she had learned how to do, who would have thought that attaching the small pin clips to her nurse's cap would be the thing to cause trouble?

"Let me help."

Ruth turned to see who had spoken. It was the woman who occupied the bunk next to hers, Helene Bizet. Ruth had noticed Helene before; it was hard not to. With stunning green eyes and cascades of dark, curly hair, the tall, graceful French woman stood out.

Helene was right behind Ruth, and an instant later, Ruth felt her hands adjusting the cap. The taller woman moved efficiently and in no time at all, Ruth's cap was perfectly situated.

"Not so hard, see?" Helene's French accent made every word sound elegant. She had both hands on Ruth's shoulders and gave a gentle squeeze.

"Thank you. I just can't seem to get the hang of those." Ruth turned to face Helene. The other woman stood very close to her and did not move back when Ruth turned.

Helene smoothed Ruth's bangs back with her cool, long fingers. She lingered on Ruth's face, touching her lightly. "I think you just needed someone to show you."

Ruth stared at Helene, who was so close that Ruth could feel her warm breath. Her body reacted to the woman's touch, a thrill of arousal delivered immediately. *Helene is like me!* Pushing down the instinct to shyly look away from the bold, older woman's gaze, Ruth held it. And then some.

"I guess I'm lucky you were here to teach me." Ruth felt her face flush, a combination of excitement and nervous embarrassment.

Helene had played this game before, many, many times. She knew as soon as Ruth had picked the bunk next to hers on that first day and later caught her staring that she was a potential lover. "I can teach you many things, *petite fleur*. Would you like that?" Helene traced the side of Ruth's face with a slow, sensuous motion.

Ruth swallowed. "Yes. Yes, I would." She could barely get the words out.

Helene dropped her hand and smiled, satisfied. "Very good." With a last smile over her shoulder, she left the room.

Ruth watched Helene's sexy walk, her full hips not able to be de-sexualized even by her nurse's garb. In that moment, Ruth knew she would happily give herself over to Helene. The sexual attraction she felt was primal and strong. Realizing that she was standing alone in the bunkroom with a silly grin on her face, she gathered her composure. It was time for her to get to work.

During the short walk to the ward room, Ruth reflected on the changes in her life. Here she was, around the world almost, at war, flirting openly with a beautiful French woman. What a difference a few months made.

Dear Mother and Pop,

Well, I'm here in merry olde England! I don't know how long it will take for this letter to get to you but I wanted to write as soon as I could once we arrived so that you wouldn't have to worry. I am doing well and am very happy to be off of the ship—Pop, I would never have made it in the Navy like you! This Carroway does not have any sea legs, that's for sure.
All of the girls I've met are swell. Everyone is a little nervous, but very friendly. Mother, I know you're angry with me for doing this but please understand that I feel like I am really doing my best to help our country, just like Frank. I've been assigned to a hospital in London and everyone says that hospitals tend to be safe.
Hope things are going well at home and that the garden is still the best on the block. I love you both.
Your daughter,
Ruth

Chapter Eleven

"Where are we going?" Ruth felt slightly nervous. Betty had told her during her brief orientation not to interfere with the senior doctor's offices. No matter how nervous she was, however, nothing could have kept her from following Helene. When Helene had whispered to Ruth that it was time for her to show her something, Ruth hadn't asked any questions. She had simply followed her. Helene was that kind of woman. She was older than Ruth and something about the way she talked, especially when her voice had been in Ruth's ear, her warm breath upon her, made Ruth weak in the knees.

"You'll see. So impatient!"

The women went down a corridor off of the main hallway. Numerous doors on either side of the corridor were closed. They appeared to be alone.

"This used to be a teaching hospital before the war. These were the professor's offices."

Ruth looked at Helene. "How do you know that?"

Helene smiled a half-smile. "I was close with one of the nursing professors. She took a…special interest in me." Helene stopped in front of one of the doors at the end of the corridor.

Ruth had a feeling she knew what the special interest in Helene was about. It made her frown but she knew that was silly. Helene was here with her now and the anticipation that Ruth was experiencing squashed any hint of jealousy. "Are you sure no one uses these anymore?"

Helene opened the door. "Only a few of us know about these offices. Everyone else is told to stay off of this floor. *Après toi*, ma cherie." She gestured for Ruth to enter.

The room wasn't in use at the moment but certainly had been used. Ruth took in the desk pushed against a wall and the small mattress squeezed in the tiny room. She looked at Helene, her eyes wide. "Do other people...come here to be alone?"

With a merry laugh, Helene closed the door behind them and turned the lock. "Only those with connections. See how lucky you are?" She sat on the mattress, her long legs extended out in front of her, and pulled a package of cigarettes from her pocket. Lighting one, she offered the package to Ruth.

"No, thank you."

"Oh, lighten up, cherie, you seem so nervous. Come sit by me."

Ruth exhaled and sat near the woman.

"So, I take it you have been with women before?" Helene asked without any preface.

"Yes. Well, one."

Helene nodded, blowing smoke in the air. Even that simple act looked sexual. "One, eh? And you liked it?"

"Oh yes. Very much." Ruth realized that she was nodding her head, enthusiastically, like a student seeking approval from a teacher.

With a low laugh, Helene stubbed out her cigarette and faced Ruth fully. "Of course you did! What's not to like, no?"

"No. I mean, yes." Ruth's face flushed with

embarrassment.

"Relax. Do not be nervous."

Ruth blew out a long breath. "I'm sorry. I just feel…"

Helene waited patiently for the rest of the sentence. It never came. "You just feel what?" she prompted gently.

"It's just that, you're so glamourous and beautiful. I feel like a silly school girl." Ruth looked at Helene for her reaction.

The reaction was swift, and telling. Helene took Ruth's face in her hands and kissed her fully on the mouth. The kiss was hungry and bold and Ruth found herself returning the energy, her own arousal growing. Helene moaned softly, causing Ruth to grow more excited. Ruth wrapped an arm around Helene and cupped her rear, squeezing it and pulling her closer as she did so. Helene moved her mouth to Ruth's neck, kissing it roughly as her breathing sped up.

"You're no school girl. When I look at you, I see a sexy, confident woman, learning how to be herself. It's wildly exciting," Helene said between kisses. After removing Ruth's shirt, she held Ruth's breast and massaged it, rolling an erect nipple between her fingers. Not leaving her breasts, Helene expertly removed Ruth's skirt and shoes and then did the same for herself.

Ruth arched back, relishing Helene's touch even as the hunger in her center began to grow. "I need you." Ruth's words came from outside of herself. It was her desire speaking now.

Helene bent her head down and gently bit Ruth's nipple, smiling at the sound it elicited from her new lover. "I will take care of you, cherie. We will take care of each other." With that, Helene pushed one of her long, slender legs between Ruth's thighs and waited just an instant for Ruth's reflexive gripping of her leg before beginning to push into her.

"Oh," Ruth cried out at the contact. "That feels good." She held Helene's head again her breast, urging her on.

Helene needed little urging. She took Ruth in her mouth and sucked, using her other hand to pleasure Ruth's exposed breast, all the while keeping time between her legs with her grinding. The sounds of Ruth's wetness soon filled the air and this made Helene even more excited. She kissed Ruth's stomach, delighting in its youthful flatness. She could feel the tension in her lover. Moving downward, she blew softly on the tuft of hair between Ruth's legs, her mouth so close to Ruth that Ruth could feel Helene's moist breath. Ruth gasped and involuntarily clenched her legs together, pushing Helene out of the way in the process.

Surprised, Helene raised up on her arms. "What's the matter, cherie?"

Ruth covered her face with her hands. "I'm sorry. I've just...I've never..."

Helene raised her eyebrows. "What? But I thought you have had a lover? Did she not please you in this way?"

Peeking out from around her hands, Ruth faced Helene. "No. We never did that. Lillian only wanted to use our hands on each other."

Helene realized then that the tension she had felt in Ruth wasn't entirely sexual, although it was certainly partly that given the wetness Helene had grazed with her fingertips. No, the tension was also that of a sexual beginner. Helene smiled. She enjoyed being the teacher in bed. Those new to the pleasures of loving a woman were such eager learners, always anxious to please their teacher. Helene had schooled more than a few women in the ways of lesbian love and had seen each leave with varying degrees of wistfulness. Looking at Ruth's shapely figure, robust as the American girls always seemed to be, Helene decided immediately that she would keep this one as long as possible. She sensed a raw sexuality under the innocence and inexperience. Once she had her body awakened, Helene knew, Ruth would be a good match for her sexually. But that would come later. Now was the time to introduce Ruth to pleasure.

Reaching up to Ruth's face, Helene gently removed Ruth's hands, kissing them tenderly. She then kissed Ruth on the mouth. Ruth hesitated at first and Helene feared that the moment had been lost. The women's bodies stretched out and matched up of their own volition, pushing against one another, seeking contact. Ruth began to respond and their kiss became passionate.

Helene broke away, leaving Ruth breathless.

"I am sorry that your lover did not want to use her mouth with you." She paused. "I am lying. I am not sorry. I am happy. This means I will be the lucky woman who has your first taste. I will be the lucky woman to introduce you to the most special kind of love between women. Do you trust me?"

Ruth looked into Helene's big green eyes, which were focused intently on her and flooded with lust. Her body answered for her. "Yes. I trust you."

Helene nodded, pleased. Without a word, she slid her long body down Ruth's and came to rest between her legs. There was no doubt of Ruth's arousal now. Dipping her head, Helene had the first taste of Ruth, earning a gasp of pleasure, which was to be the first of many. Helene's experience, both in skill and in reading the signs of a woman's body, was Ruth's boon. Ruth could not take her eyes off of Helene and watched as the other woman brought her to heights of ecstasy that she had never known were possible. When Helene looked up at Ruth while pleasing her, Ruth felt a swell of arousal, contentment, and physical pleasure that threatened to overwhelm her. She found herself clutching Helene's hair, pushing her deeper all while thrusting her hips upward.

Helene was tireless in her efforts and upon feeling Ruth grab her hair in the throes of passion, moaned with her own sexual desire. She was thrilled to have unlocked such animalism in Ruth so soon and felt the familiar sense of proud sexual prowess as she made Ruth climax. Reaching between her own legs to satisfy her urgent need, she felt not an ounce of dissatisfaction. She was willing to wait for the time when Ruth would make love to her. She was willing to wait because she knew that the wait would be worth it.

᠅᠅᠅᠅

The women's barracks held a small common area for socializing. It wasn't much. A well-used wicker table and chair set, a phonograph and a stack of albums, and a few mismatched extra chairs made up the recreational stores. But it wasn't the fixtures that made the room the center of the nurses' downtime—it was the opportunity to congregate for brief periods of time without the sometimes domineering male surgeons around, the freedom to laugh with their fellow women and the illusion, however brief, that they were not in the middle of a war. As a result, the room was in use nearly round-the-clock, accommodating the nurses who worked each shift, and all were welcome.

Ruth sat at the table with five other off-duty nurses. Three of the women were military nurses and wore their off-duty uniforms, while Ruth and the others relaxed in civilian clothes. The nurses reveled in the chance to wear apparel from home and the casual sweaters and slacks allowed them to escape their reality, even if only for a short time.

The last of the women retired for the night, leaving Ruth with just the lingering cigarette smoke and echoes of their laughter. She knew she should leave and head to bed as well. Morning would come all too soon. But something about the quiet of the small common room held her. She idly flipped through an outdated Time magazine, one of several that littered the table. Re-reading the magazine didn't hold her interest and she soon pushed it across the table. She stretched her arms over her head.

Six months ago, Ruth had been across the Atlantic, cloistered in her small town and its small minds, with her heart broken by her first love. Now, she felt that she had lived several lifetimes and had seen more than she had ever dreamed was possible. An ocean, another country, people from all over the world, wartime atrocities, death too many times over, it was almost too much to fathom. She had grown up. Thinking back to her life in Evansville, those days frolicking on the beach, no wonder the "elders" had chastised her. She had been a child in a woman's body. Even her love affair with Lillian had been immature in many ways.

Reflecting on their time together, Ruth realized they had simply been experimenting with love, playing "house."

Thoughts of Lillian and her first lovemaking experiences with a woman naturally brought Ruth's mind to the present and to Helene. Ah, Helene. With Helene, Ruth certainly did not feel like a child. It had been four weeks since their first experience together and in that time, they had stolen numerous other opportunities to make love. When Helene and Ruth were together, Ruth knew what it meant to be a woman who loved women and she thanked God for it. Not for the first time, Ruth wondered if she ever would have learned the things that Helene had shown her if not for the war. Also not for the first time, Ruth felt a gnawing guilt for the flash for gratitude toward the war that had brought her this new life, this new freedom, and of course, Helene. There was so much to ponder and so much of it was so troublesome. Sometimes, it was better not to ponder at all.

Chapter Twelve

"Who's the new girl?" Ruth asked as she watched Betty talk to a woman who was dragging a footlocker behind her.

"That's Tess Davies. English girl. Probably a cold fish; they all are," Midgie said with a dismissive nod. Midgie, besides being a smart and funny woman, always seemed to know the latest gossip.

"What do you mean?"

"You are an innocent, aren't you, hon?" Midgie said with a laugh. "I just mean that English girls can be a little stand-offish."

Ruth looked again at Tess. She was about Ruth's height, which was to say, not very tall. Her eyes were a deep brown and her hair, cut short, was also a dark brown. With high cheekbones and a purposeful posture, she made quite an impression. The woman must have felt the stare because she looked up and met Ruth's eyes. With a perfunctory nod, she acknowledged Ruth and then returned to her orientation briefing.

The sight of another new arrival brought Ruth back to her first day. Had it only been two months ago? So much had happened since then. She had always wanted to return the favor that Midgie had done, helping her settle in, to another new nurse but this nurse didn't seem to need any help at all. She was nodding to Betty as Betty apparently finished her briefing and left the room.

Ruth watched Tess's progress with interest. She was pulling the trunk behind her, looking from side to side at the room. There were two beds open, one close to Ruth's bunk and the other at the opposite end. Not sure why, Ruth hoped that the new nurse would choose the bunk nearby. *What would the new girl think of the sounds that Helene and I make?* Ruth wondered as a naughty tingle made its way through her body. Some of the other nurses had teased the two of them when their nighttime exploits got a little loud, despite their attempt to make a privacy screen with clotheslines and blankets. Other nurses obviously disapproved but simply moved to bunks further away.

Ruth wondered if Midgie was right. Was she a cold fish?

༄༄༄༄

"Boy, they can powder anything, can't they?" Midgie asked, her fork limp over another desultory meal in the mess hall. "Powdered eggs, powdered milk, you name it."

"Don't be a complainer, Midgie," Shorty teased. "There's canned fruit at least. Look at these beautiful peaches." She speared a peach on a fork and held it in the air for emphasis.

Ruth laughed with the rest of them. Despite the setting, she loved being with the other women. The camaraderie they shared was like a comfortable blanket to settle around your shoulders. "If you could have any meal, what would it be?" she asked. The women often played the game, although it served more to tantalize them than anything. Even so, it was a fun way to pass time.

"A big, juicy steak," Ruby said right away. She was a Texas girl and lived on a cattle farm back home.

"Mmm, yes! With some fresh tomatoes from the garden, still warm from the sun."

Others joined in eagerly, creating an imaginary meal that they would never eat.

"Corn on the cob, too. With lots of butter and salt."

"My mother's fresh biscuits. Nothing like the little hard bricks they serve us."

"What about you, Tess?" Ruby asked, trying to include the silent English woman into the conversation. "What would you pick?"

Tess looked up from her coffee. "I don't imagine that pretending I can have food that I certainly cannot have does anything but remind me that I cannot have it. I don't want to play, thank you."

Ruby frowned. The women fell silent, awkward after Tess's comment. Ruth decided to continue on and ignore the statement rather than make a fuss. "And dessert, don't forget dessert. How about a big chocolate cake, lots of frosting?"

The women groaned. Sweets were in short supply and universally craved.

Ruth completed the "meal." "Topped with ice cream, delicious ice cream."

Some of the women clapped at the thought. Ice cream hadn't been seen for a very long time. With it brought images of carefree summer days, perhaps holding hands during a walk with a beau. Tess's grumpy opinion had been forgotten.

Ruth stole a glance at Tess, who was focused on her coffee and seemed not to care that she was making herself more and more of an outsider. She wondered what went on in her head and imagined her eating a more civilized breakfast. Probably tea served in fine china and crumpets with jam. She was certainly an enigma.

The powdered breakfast continued on.

≈≈≈≈

After breakfast, Ruth headed to the hospital areas. Her confidence in her skills had grown. She *could* make a difference. She *did* know what she was doing. She *would* help. After all, wasn't that why she was here?

Triage was worse than the OR. With triage, one never knew what one would find on that gurney. It could be a simple flesh wound or a gruesome head injury. You never wanted to show any shock or revulsion when you first encountered a patient. While many were unconscious, many were not. Ruth knew that the comfort of a woman's voice and a gentle hand on the chest during the initial examination could make the unthinkable a little easier to bear. At least that's what she told herself. Given the looks of appreciation she often got, thankful eyes of young men with shattered bodies, she thought she was probably right.

The day's latest wounded, however, would need more than gentle touches and kind words. Whatever battle they had come from had been especially fierce. There were dozens of men on litters, taking up every available spot in the hallways of the hospital and more kept flowing in, making keeping up impossible. Even the more experienced nurses wore grim faces of worry and stress as they moved from man to man, trying to determine which men needed treatment first.

Ruth knelt beside a soldier who was groaning and holding his stomach, which leaked blood despite the field bandages that had been applied. She noticed a mark on his forehead. It looked like the letter "M" had been written on him. Confused, she looked at the patient on the opposite side of the hall. He too had a letter written on his forehead but this time it was the letter "T."

"Helene," Ruth said as the Frenchwoman hurried through, her arms full of medical supplies.

"Yes?" Helene's voice was all business but her eyes were kind. They always were for Ruth.

"These letters. An M on this one and a T on the other. What does it mean? Have they been assigned to certain doctors?"

Helene smiled. "No, cherie. M means the patient needs morphine. T means tetanus. The medics in the field have no time for charts so they make do." Helene continued walking quickly toward the other end of the hall with her supplies but turned over her shoulder as she did so. "You're learning, cherie, don't worry!"

Ruth nodded, filing away the tidbit with the seeming endless amount of new information she gathered each day. She worked with the first man, administering morphine, which was immediately effective and brought her a smile of immense gratitude from the recipient. The young soldier had a gap between his teeth that made him seem impossibly young. But then, Ruth thought, she probably seemed just as young to her patients.

She moved to the next gurney, empowered by her work. She knelt beside the man, a dark-haired fellow with his eyes closed. "Soldier, I'm Nurse Carroway," she said softly, feeling a burst of pride. She was making a difference, one patient at a time. She felt for the man's vitals and frowned. Nothing. Maybe she was feeling in the wrong place. She tried again and felt nothing. A sweat formed in an instant on Ruth's brow. She looked again at the man's face and noticed that his mouth was slightly open, as were his eyes. Peeling at one of the eyes, she saw the lifeless, brown eyes, fixed in place. The man was dead.

Ruth leaned back on her heels and stared at the newly deceased. Had he ever had a chance? Did her exchange with Helene cost the few seconds that might have saved his life? Ruth knew it was unlikely but still, the unpleasant feeling persisted. The poor boy. He had a family somewhere that didn't know he was dead. In fact, at that exact moment in time, Ruth realized, she was the only person in the world who knew that this man, this PFC David Williams per his dogtags, was not coming home, not ever.

The loud cry from a nearby soldier shook Ruth from her reverie. She was needed. She couldn't help PFC Williams, but perhaps could help the others. Saying a silent prayer and pulling a sheet over the still-warm man, Ruth moved on.

Chapter Thirteen

Nights were the hardest. The bunkroom was always cold and invariably one or the other of the nurses would be coming from or going to a nighttime shift. The beds were not plush but simply served the utilitarian purpose of a place to lay your head. There was no sense of real privacy and no place to call your own beyond the tiny twin bed and the footlocker at its end. And always, always there was the tension of being ready for the alert signal that all nurses were needed to tend to a new batch of shredded young men after a particularly brutal battle.

Ruth lay in her bed and considered how different her world here in England was from Evansville. If she closed her eyes, she might pretend she was in her own comfortable bedroom, with her childhood things surrounding her, her family down the hall, her entire world within the square mileage of the city. In Evansville, the only dangers were the occasional gossip and perhaps an auto accident. Not like here, where things were truly life or death each day.

Thinking of Helene and of the freedom she had to be with her, Ruth knew, though, that Evansville had its own kind of danger and that danger had been smothering Ruth. The inability to be herself, to explore the sexuality that was in fact so central to who she was becoming and was meant to be—was that not a danger that threatened Ruth as much as the bombs of London?

The sound of soft crying interrupted Ruth's thoughts. One of the nurses crying at night was not unusual, not at all. The things that the women saw daily were enough to bring any of them to tears, even after being hardened by war. And of course, there was the loneliness, the separation from boyfriends, fiancés, and families. Along with that, the inevitable string of notifications of loved ones lost to the war, as had been the case in the Great War and every war prior to that. No, there was no shortage of reasons for the women to weep into their pillows before drifting off into exhausted sleep in the bunkroom. It wasn't the fact that someone was crying that grabbed Ruth's attention—it was the fact that it was Tess.

The "cold fish" Tess, who the other nurses thought to be hard and unreachable, was softly weeping in the bunk next to Ruth. Ruth could make out Tess's form, with her back turned towards her. Eyes wide open and fully awake, Ruth stared in the darkness at the beautiful, if enigmatic, woman who had been slowly drawing her in. Every piece of her wanted to cross the few feet between their bunks and crawl into the bed with Tess. Ruth could imagined herself fitting her body behind the other woman's and wrapping her arms around her, holding her close and taking her pain from her, even if for just a moment. A wave of emotion and tenderness swept through Ruth with such power that it nearly lifted Ruth from her bed to put her imaginings into action.

But Ruth stayed in her own bunk. The distance between the two women might well have been the ocean that divided their home countries. Her instincts told her not to push, not yet. Instead, Ruth took the lumpy pillow from beneath her head and held it in her arms, her Tess for now.

※ ※ ※ ※

The next morning, Ruth awoke to see Tess efficiently making her bed, having already dressed in her nurse's uniform. Her eyes were dry and her face impassive. She gave no clue that she had been the vulnerable woman of the night, alone and crying. Now, she was the Tess that all of the others knew—the no-nonsense, "typical" English hard case. Ruth felt a tingle of excitement…and something more, because she now had a glimpse of a different side of Tess. If only she could find out the rest.

※ ※ ※ ※

"Man on the floor!" a nurse yelled.

The nurses glanced to the door of their bunkroom, more curious than alarmed. They saw not a man but Gabriel in the doorway, his eyes wide and a sweet grin spread across his face. He was eight years old, an English boy orphaned in one instant by the cursed war, his parents obliterated in a bombing raid. Their only son had been out of the house, spared a violent death only to be left parentless. All of the nurses knew Gabriel; he was a sweet boy who eked out an existence by begging for food from the most reliable source—the good-hearted nurses of the hospital. He was a bright spot in an often dreadful existence. Ruth especially had taken an interest in the boy.

Ruby, a bosomy woman from deep Texas, carried on the tease. "Oh no, it's a man in here with all of these ladies!"

Several of the women played along, emitting faux cries of alarm. Gabriel's smile threatened to wrap around his head.

"It's not a man! It's me!" he said with a laugh.

The nurses swarmed the young boy, showering him with hugs. Their hearts broke for his plight, a boy orphaned suddenly in the most horrific manner possible (right in front of his own eyes some said in hushed tones). But they always welcomed his presence in the bunkroom. When Gabriel was around, it was easy to pretend there wasn't a war going on outside, that perhaps the sweet, polite boy was a young brother or cousin at a family gathering where the biggest concern was whether the lemonade stayed cold and there was enough potato salad. Everyone engaged in these fictions; it was necessary to keep one's sanity and good spirits.

Ruth reached into her footlocker to retrieve a candy bar that she had been saving for Gabriel. A pilot at the bar who thought he might improve his chances with Ruth by offering sweets had given it to her. Little had he known that he had never had a chance at all. In any event, the chocolate bar would be a special treat for the boy and Ruth had been looking forward to seeing him to reveal the treasure.

Gabriel made his way around the room, the nurses hugging him, many of whom had food for him. When he got to Ruth, he dove into her arms. "Miss Ruth!"

Ruth squeezed the boy tightly. Having never had a little brother, she liked to imagine that he was hers. She felt a strong affection for him and had asked the other nurses, more than once, if they couldn't invite Gabriel to stay on in the bunkroom on a permanent basis. The others had talked her out of it, saying that Gabriel had mentioned an aunt in the city. Ruth doubted that there was an aunt but it was too painful to think of Gabriel completely alone out there, just a small child. So, she allowed herself to believe that he did indeed go home to a loving aunt. Another of the necessary fictions needed to stay sane.

Chapter Fourteen

*D*ear Frank,

I hope you're doing okay. I haven't gotten a letter from you yet but it seems mail gets back home faster than it can be delivered here. Things here in London are, well, you know how it is. I feel like I can tell you things that I don't tell Mother and Pop in my letters. I don't want to worry them but I know you will understand. I'm sure you've seen lots worse than I have.

Nursing isn't what I thought it would be. I suppose I was thinking of Nurse Grandy, remember her? The nurse at Doctor Albert's office? She was always nice and took our temperature before giving us a lollipop. I don't think Nurse Grandy would like nursing over here. I've never seen so much blood or so many people in pain. It gets to you. You wonder if you could do more. Sometimes you get so angry that any of this is happening you feel like you might explode. Do you ever feel like that, Frank?

Of all the patients I've seen, I never thought I'd see one from home. But, yesterday, I did. Well, not quite home. This boy wasn't from Evansville but his family's farm is only twenty miles from town so it's practically like

home. We talked a little bit after he got out of surgery. It looked like he was going to make it, but he didn't. He was only nineteen. In my mind, I tell myself that only one soldier from Evansville could die. I think you know Gerald Reed—well, he was killed. Now this young man has died. I don't think anyone else from Evansville will die; it would just be too many. So, I think you're safe. I sure hope so.
    Love,
    Ruth*

Ruth re-read the letter and closed her eyes, thinking of her handsome brother. She crumpled up the letter and threw it away.

꧁꧂

Ruth looked forward to a beer, even though she knew it would be warm. It had been a tough shift and her body hurt from the physicality of her work. Every fiber of her ached for a nap. Instead, she was on her way for a drink. Beer...yet another change for her since she came overseas. She had had a few drinks at home, once at a party, a couple of times at a bar when on a date. But more typically, she asked for a ginger ale with a lime. She hadn't liked the feeling of losing control, nor had she wanted to face the disapproving looks of her mother on the rare occasion that she came home with alcohol on her breath. Never mind that Frank got tight with his friends on most weekends. All that happened to him was a wry smile and a comment to the effect of boys will be boys. But here, abroad and at war, Ruth had developed a taste for beer. Or, more accurately, a taste for the feelings that beer produced. She was an adult now, in every sense.

The beer alone didn't pull Ruth to the makeshift bar that nurses and doctors often frequented when there was a break in the chaos. The camaraderie, looseness, relaxation, and freedom were powerful draws. It was at the bar that Helene had first put her arm around Ruth in public. The idea of others seeing them together as more than friends had thrilled Ruth. It felt dangerous, but also liberating. There had been no kissing or slow dancing at the bar; that would have been too much. But Helene had stayed close to Ruth on the occasions that they went together, pushing their bar stools together, dancing the Lindy Hop with her on the grimy dance floor. When she did these things, Ruth experienced a sensation of pride that was new to her. Helene was "claiming" her and it felt deliciously exciting.

Ruth had felt that excitement as she walked into the bar after a shift, looking for Helene. The excitement evaporated immediately when she spotted the French woman, already at the bar but with another woman. This time it was Helene and the stranger pushed together tightly, laughing over a shared joke, arms casually draped on the back of the other.

The other woman was attractive, beautiful even. She wore a flight nurse's jacket and had short, curly hair that framed a strong, aquiline-featured face. Even from across the bar, Ruth recognized the flirtatious long stares, the laughter that went on longer than usual, the undeniable connection. This was no "new nurse friend," Ruth realized immediately with a newfound sense of jealously and possessiveness. This was competition.

Helene held a cigarette between two long fingers and looked expectantly at her companion. Ruth's stomach clenched when she saw the flight nurse extract matches from her jacket and light Helene's cigarette. The act was sensual, laden with the promise of sex. Blinking back tears of indignation, Ruth made her way to the bar.

"Beer, love?" Stan asked. Stan had lost a leg in the First World War and in some sort of odd calculus, now made a fair living serving drinks to the Second World War's soldiers, doctors, and nurses. His suggestion of a beer wasn't a function of Ruth being a regular. He had beer or whiskey and the young woman didn't look like she was ready for whiskey. *Although another year in this kind of hell may change that*, Stan thought to himself. His smile stayed fixed, not revealing his thoughts. On another man, the thoughts might have been cynical, but Stan had been there. He knew what war was.

Ruth perched primly on a stool two down from Helene and her partner. She avoided looking toward the women but smiled sweetly at Stan. "That would be swell." She purposely talked louder than was necessary, wanting to be sure that Helene knew she was there. It worked.

"Cherie, hello," Helene said in a syrupy voice.

Ruth recognized the slight slur of too much alcohol. She turned to look at Helene, as if surprised to see her.

"Oh, hello." With a pointed stare at the flight nurse, Ruth surprised herself with the boldness of her next words. "Who's your friend?"

"This is Margo. She's a flight nurse." Helene smiled, seeming to enjoy the moment. The way she said "flight nurse" made clear that she was impressed with Margo and expected Ruth to feel the same.

Margo offered a broad smile to Ruth, not putting together the pieces, not realizing that she was right in the middle of two lovers. "Nice to meet you. Like she said, I'm Margo."

"Ruth," Ruth responded with an edge. She couldn't help but stare at Margo. She really was striking. Her features were strong and the way she carried herself…there was something about it. She wore her flight jacket open in the front to reveal an ample chest. *Why can't she put that jacket on a stool? I know why, because she's showing off.* When Margo looked back at Ruth, her eyes holding Ruth's, Ruth knew that she was starting to get the picture.

"You two know each other, I take it?" Margo looked from Ruth to Helene.

Helene exhaled a mouthful of smoke. "Ruth and I are, how do you say, special friends. We enjoy one another."

Ruth's face flamed. Helene's characterization of their relationship felt cheap, crass even. Was that all they were? *Special friends?*

Margo turned to Helene, moving her stool close. With one arm draped possessively around Helene's back, she spoke directly to Helene. "Well, how could a girl not enjoy a woman like you?"

Helene laughed, a lilting, flirtatious laugh of a woman who knew she was desired. "You're too sweet, cherie."

Ruth frowned at Helene's use of the endearment. It was clear that Margo had her sights on Helene. Was Helene really going to treat Ruth this way? Her mind raced through several things to say, but her mouth couldn't catch up before Margo spoke again.

"First time, hon?" She leaned in toward Ruth and winked before throwing back a long drink of beer.

"Don't tease the poor girl, Margo," Helene said, without much conviction. She swatted Margo's arm but left her hand there.

Helene's dismissiveness made tears of hurt and embarrassment rush to Ruth's eyes. Without another word, she took the beer that Stan had placed in front of her and got up from the bar.

Not wanting to appear completely cowed, she resisted the urge to flee entirely and looked around for a familiar face, someone to sit with. She found that someone in the form of one Tess Davies, sitting alone at a table with a short glass of something dark and clear in front of her.

"Mind if I join you?" Ruth asked, forcing her voice to remain even. She didn't wait for an answer before sitting down at the small table.

"Well, I suppose American manners are a bit different than those I'm used to. Isn't it customary for one to receive an invitation before sitting?"

"I'm sorry. I don't mean to intrude but I just need a friend right now." Ruth surprised herself with the candor of her own statement and expected Tess to tell her exactly where to go.

"Hmm. Well, cheers then." Tess raised her glass to Ruth, without looking at her.

Ruth cautiously clinked her glass to Tess's, wondering if perhaps the other woman was drunk. The two sat without talking, each nursing their drink. Finally, Tess spoke again.

"I've heard you, you know." Tess kept her eyes in her drink.

"Heard me?"

"With the tall one. The French girl?" Still, Tess did not look at Ruth.

Ruth realized at once what she was talking about. She had heard Helene and Ruth making love. Of course! After all, their bunks were so close and many times, well, Helene was a skilled lover and Ruth had learned that she herself was not able to be quiet when the moment overtook her. "Oh. I see."

"I'm not a prude as the others would have you believe."

Ruth swirled her beer in her glass. Not quite sure how to respond, she said nothing.

"I've had a girlfriend myself. So, don't mind the rumors about English being cold fish." At last, Tess looked over. Her stern words didn't match her expression. She was looking for a friend, too. She was looking for someone who would understand.

"You've had a girlfriend?" Ruth repeated.

"That's right. Surprised?"

In truth, Ruth was surprised…and thrilled. She had been watching Tess and realizing a growing attraction for her but had never imagined that something might come of it. As her mind raced with the new information, Ruth stumbled over a response. "Well, no, I mean, sort of."

Tess returned to her drink. "I suppose you thought only French girls could do such a thing?"

"No, no. That's not it." Ruth realized she was staring at Tess, seeing her in a whole new light. Now that there was an actual possibility of an interaction. Ruth's crush had turned into longing in ten seconds flat.

"Well, what then?" Tess's tone sounded irritated,

but it was forced. She was anxious to know what Ruth thought. She'd heard Ruth and Helene more than once, their soft moans, heavy sighs, giggles, and other sounds of lovemaking. Lying awake, she'd tried not to pay attention but found that she was mesmerized. The American girl was so different from Tess, so carefree and easygoing. And beautiful.

"I just didn't expect it of you, that's all." Ruth stared at Tess, willing her to make eye contact. She did. Both of them softened a bit. "So, what happened? You said you 'had' a girlfriend. Did you break her heart?" Ruth smiled, trying to break the tension. It didn't work.

"How about we talk about something else? Such as you buying me a drink for letting you sit here?" Tess offered a smile at last.

"Of course." Ruth knew it was a good idea to back off, for now. Besides, seeing that smile was more than worth the price of a drink.

※※※※

The women chatted about their lives before the war, their status as younger sisters (both had brothers), and the quality of food in the mess. They were still enjoying each other's company and bantering when a third woman appeared at their table. It was Helene and she was beyond tipsy.

"Well, isn't this cozy?" she cooed.

Ruth realized that her earlier jealousy about the flight nurse had cooled, but only somewhat. "Where's your friend?"

Helene raised her eyebrows. "Margo? She had to run. We're meeting up later." She looked pointedly at Ruth. "Unless you prefer to spend some time with me?"

Tess studied her drink, its contents suddenly having become fascinating.

Ruth felt embarrassed. She didn't want Tess to see her this way, being second choice for Helene's night of conquests. "No, I'm quite happy here."

Helene made a tsk-tsk sound with her lips. "I see. Well, you may not get another chance to see me tonight if you don't want to go now." She looked at Ruth, daring her to refuse.

Before Ruth could respond, Tess interrupted. "I wonder when you'll realize that you're the only one who thinks of yourself as magnificent." Her crisp diction was in stark contrast to Helene's slightly slurred words.

Helene glared at Tess for a long moment before allowing the glare to dissolve into a cruel smile. "*Formidable*," she said in French. "It looks like the cold fish has a heartbeat after all. Intriguing." The look that Helene gave Tess was one that was hard to decipher—angry? Bemused? Aroused? Perhaps all three. Without another word, Helene strode off.

Ruth felt a quick rush of emotion that took her a moment to identify properly. Jealousy. She was jealous. But of which woman?

Chapter Fifteen

Dear Ruth,

I imagine you're surprised to get a letter from me. I've been wanting to write this letter practically from the moment I saw you last but was too proud. I had a dream last night that you were injured over there and when I woke up, I decided that I needed to write this letter, my pride be damned!

I am truly sorry for the things I said and did after Gerald died. I could blame it on the shock of losing my husband but that would just be an excuse. There's really no excuse for my behavior and I am ashamed. I hope you can forgive me.

Please know that our time together was more special to me that I can ever express. I hope that when you get back home that you will find it in your heart to speak to me. I feel as if there is so much more to say.

For now, I hope you're safe and that you get back soon.

Yours,
Lillian

Ruth re-read the letter and then read it a third time. The letter was completely unexpected, and when

Ruth had first spotted the familiar loopy handwriting that she knew was Lillian's, she had wondered if Lillian was writing her a nasty letter. She certainly wouldn't have imagined that Lillian would pen the words that she had, not after their last encounters.

Sitting back, Ruth folded the letter carefully and returned it to its envelope, creased and mangled after its trans-Atlantic passage. When she was in Staten Island and even in her first few weeks in London, receiving a letter like this would have been a dream come true for Ruth. She had mooned over Lillian and cried endless tears about the break-up. Once she met Helene and started whatever they had started, she had rarely given Lillian a thought. There was no doubting the intent of the letter, though. Lillian seemed to have realized that she was made for women, not men. And Ruth, a comfortable and safe woman, was the first thing that came to her mind.

Ruth stared at the postmark as her thoughts meandered. She explored whether she felt anything upon receiving the letter. Did she have unresolved feelings about Lil? Would she rush back into her arms when she got home? Was she too seeking the safety of the known?

"So, you've made a new friend, I see." Helene's voice was patronizing, but there was an edge to it as well.

The women were finishing up getting into their uniforms, preparing for another day. Ruth was headed for an inventory shift with Tess, which she was looking forward to. She wanted the opportunity to talk with her again and besides, inventory duty was the most stress-free of any of the nursing tasks.

"What do you mean?" Ruth asked without looking up. She asked even though she knew exactly what Helene meant. She wanted to hear her say Tess's name, to know that seeing Ruth with another woman had had some effect on her.

"The English girl. Tess I think her name is?"

"Yes, we've become friendly." Ruth continued ironing her uniform, not looking up at Helene. She could smell the smoke from Helene's ever-present cigarette. The smell reminded her of the taste of Helene's mouth and sent a confusing ripple of desire through her.

"Oh? How friendly, cherie?"

Helene was standing closer now and Ruth could feel her presence. Helene was a powerful and sexual woman and she seemed to exude sensuality.

"Does it matter?"

"Don't be coy; it does not suit you. I am just curious. We are lovers, are we not?"

Ruth's instinct was to look around. Had anyone heard? The other nurses largely ignored the pursuits behind the curtain but still... She took in Helene. God, she was beautiful. "We are lovers, yes. But what about Margo? Are you *friendly* with her?"

Helene laughed. "So, that is what this is about. You are jealous." She took one step backward and crossed her arms, lifting her cigarette to her lips again. "It is sweet, you being jealous."

"Aren't you?" Ruth regretted the words instantly. She didn't want Helene to have the upper hand in this conversation but there was no denying it now. Ruth had given voice to her insecurity and she knew that made Helene more powerful.

"Jealous?" Another laugh. "Of the cold fish? I don't think so." Helene stepped forward again and raised Ruth's chin gently with one hand, bringing Ruth's eyes level to her own. "I know how to make you feel good. And I am very good at that. So, what do I have to be jealous of?"

With a light kiss on Ruth's lips, Helene turned on one heel and left. She didn't look back.

In contrast, Ruth could not keep her eyes from Helene's long, retreating figure. Helene was right. She knew how to make Ruth feel good. Even now, the physical closeness and the tense dynamic of their conversation had left Ruth with a racing heart and a desirous body. She shook her head and left for duty.

✻✻✻✻

"Do you ever think about trying again?"

Tess didn't look up from her review of the medicine cart. "You'll have to be more specific."

"A woman. Being with another woman."

Tess turned her head sharply at the comment, clearly not expecting it. "I suppose you Americans don't keep talk at the pub simply talk at the pub."

Ruth wasn't going to give up. "We Americans like to get to know one another. And this American is just making conversation, trying to get to know you better, that's all."

Tess returned to the inventory with a small huff. "Why would you want to get to know me better? We're nurses assigned to the same hospital. When the war ends, soon, God willing, we will return to our lives and never see each other again. What's the point of investing energy in getting to know one another?"

The response was delivered with a dismissive air.

Ruth, for the first time, truly saw Tess as a cold fish. She stayed silent, counting bottles of medicine and willing the embarrassed flush to go away quickly.

A few moments later, Tess murmured something intelligible.

"What's that?" Ruth asked.

Tess exhaled, irritated. "I said I don't think about trying again. If you must know."

Ruth put her clipboard down, relieved that Tess wasn't going to leave their conversation so awkwardly truncated. "But why? Aren't you lonely? Don't you want to be in love again...knowing how it feels?"

The information that Tess had just jotted down on her sheet suddenly became very interesting. She stared hard at the paper and Ruth could see her jaw was clenched. But not in anger. She seemed to be holding back emotion.

"Of course I get lonely. I'm human, which some of you Americans think must not be possible for the English. But I'll take loneliness over the pain I felt after...Rose. Loneliness you get used to."

"I understand," Ruth said, although in reality, she didn't. How could a woman as young and intelligent as Tess simply call it quits on love...forever? She knew she should let the subject drop but she couldn't. "I don't know what happened with Rose and it's none of my business, but whatever it was, it doesn't mean it would happen again."

Tess looked at Ruth and examined her earnest, open face. "But it might. And I can't bear that again."

Ruth instinctually touched Tess's arm. It was a gentle touch and conveyed with it a wealth of emotion: sorrow, warmth, empathy, affection. To her surprise, Tess did not pull away but instead offered her a slight smile. "You could take a chance," Ruth said, trying again.

"I'm not the gambling type."

※.※!※.※

The next day was a Saturday, but that didn't mean a day off. The war didn't run on a business calendar. Ruth had pulled laundry duty and was struggling with a pile of bed linens in the ward. As a Red Cross nurse, she knew that she was expected to help wherever needed and that the work wasn't always as exciting as it could be in the operating room. Some days, like this one, she was called upon to do more menial tasks. She tried not to think about the fact that some of the bed linens in her arms had been covering the deathbeds of young soldiers. *Think of the boys who are saved*, she reminded herself. It was small solace when she literally was holding the sheets that had last held young men who were now dead.

"Heavy load?"

Ruth turned in the direction of the words and frowned inwardly when she identified their source. It was Doctor Rahn. The man may have been a physician and an Army officer, but he acted more coarsely than any working man Ruth had encountered back home. She had witnessed him speaking patronizingly to other nurses more often than not, his words laden with condescension for the women's work, position, and gender itself. The only other way he was apparently capable of speaking to women was in a tone that made clear that what he wanted from you had nothing to do with your efficiency in the operating ward or your compassionate care of the boys. No, this man thought women were on this earth only to serve him, either in his capacity as a surgeon or in his bed.

"It's not more than I can manage, Doctor," Ruth said with what she hoped was a confident smile that would send him on his way.

It was not.

"You sure? You're so small, not like some of the other war horse nurses around here." His appraising look, which had nothing to do with determining if she needed assistance with the load, made Ruth feel dirty.

"No, really. I'm fine, thank you."

The man closed the distance between them in three long steps and was so close to Ruth that she could smell the liquor on his breath. She felt a quick pulse of fear as she realized that what she assumed would just be an annoying encounter had suddenly escalated to a potentially dangerous one. Hefting her load to readjust the weight, Ruth moved to the doctor's right to get out of his direct line of sight.

"What's the hurry, sweetheart? The war's not going anywhere. You're Carroway, right? I've seen you around the operating room, always scurrying here and there."

Irritation partially subsumed the rush of danger Ruth had felt. She didn't like being referred to as someone who "scurried." She was a Red Cross nurse, damn it, and proud of her role. "Yes, I'm Carroway. Nurse Carroway to be precise." As soon as the words were out of her mouth, Ruth regretted them. Why had she provoked him? Why couldn't she hold her tongue, as her mother had so often advised?

Doctor Rahn laughed. There was nothing merry or jovial about the sound. Instead, it had a cruel tone. "A feisty one, huh? I like that." Rahn grabbed Ruth's shoulders, rather roughly, and pulled her as close to him as the intervening pile of linens would allow.

Ruth stared at the hands on her, noting the size. A flitter of a question, wholly irrelevant given the circumstances, rushed through her mind. How could a man with such bulky ham hands perform surgery? Weren't surgeons supposed to have delicate, graceful hands? Not these clubbish appendages that were holding her in place.

"I need to go, Doctor," Ruth said, not making eye contact. She was afraid of looking at him, afraid that she might see exactly what she was afraid of.

"And *I* said, what's your hurry, kid?" With one quick swat, Rahn pushed the awkward pile from Ruth's hands, leaving it in a dirty tumble on the floor. "That's better. Let me get a look at you."

Shocked by the sudden movement, Ruth reflexively looked up and immediately wished she hadn't. The man had eyes that meant only trouble for her. Confirming the smell of booze were his glassy, red eyes, which were nearly squinting at her as he roamed her body visually.

"Definitely not like the old war horses. No, you're more like a young, wild filly. One that looks like she needs to be ridden hard and broken." With that, he pulled Ruth close to him, so close that she felt his erection against her uniform.

"Doctor! Please!" Ruth cried. She was terrified. Somehow, she had found herself in a very dangerous position: alone and vulnerable with a drunken, rough beast.

"You don't have to beg, sweetheart. I know what you need." Rahn pressed her mouth on Ruth's, his wet, liquor breath in her face and his beard stubble scraping her cheek. "I need it, too."

Ruth twisted her head sharply, trying to wrest his mouth from hers, her arms still immobilized by his tight grip.

"Don't fight me." Rahn's words sounded like a growl. He continued to push himself into Ruth, every point of contact unwanted and repulsive.

"What's going on here?" The woman's voice came from the doorway of the room. It was commanding and demanded an answer.

"What the hell?" Rahn muttered, loosening his grasp for just the instant that Ruth needed to wrench free.

Taking several steps backward on unsteady feet, Ruth felt relief course through her body. She looked to her rescuer, who stood like a general, hands on hips. It was Tess.

"I said, what's going on here, Doctor?" Despite her stature, Tess's presence was large, large enough to make an impact on Rahn, who blinked several times.

"Nurse Davies. About time you got here. You need to report this one to the head nurse. This one threw herself at me like a common whore. What kind of discipline does your crew operate under, anyway?" Rahn's indignation was somewhat muted by his slurring of his words and of course, by the truth.

Ruth bristled immediately. *Common whore? Threw herself at him?* "How dare you!" She felt a fury more intense than she'd ever experienced. She moved a step in his direction, only for Tess to stop her.

"Carroway! That's enough," Tess barked. "It seems the doctor was just on his way out." She glared at Rahn, who seemed to have sobered up quickly.

"Keep the staff in order, Nurse, or I'll make sure you're wiping up bed pans," Rahn said as he walked toward the door. He made a show of a long, angry stare at Ruth before exiting.

As soon as he was out of the door, Tess's mood shifted. She held Ruth by the shoulders. "Are you okay, Ruth?"

Ruth was stunned. The near attack, the verbal accusations from Rahn, Tess's sudden appearance, and now a glimpse of her warm side. Not to mention, it was the first time Tess had ever called Ruth by her first name. The adrenaline rush subsided and Ruth felt weak. She trembled briefly and felt Tess's hands tighten on her, holding her steady.

"You've had quite a scare. That ass." Tess glared in the direction that Rahn had gone. "You okay, then?" Tess's voice was soft, full of concern and very different than Ruth had ever heard it in the other venues—the operating room, triage, the bunk hall. This was a new Tess. Or perhaps the same Tess, just showing herself at last?

"I don't know," Ruth said honestly. She looked into Tess's worried eyes and felt a wall fall. Her own wall. Tears immediately filled and then spilled from her eyes. She buried her head in Tess's shoulder. To her surprise, Tess did not balk. Instead, she stroked Ruth's hair and held her closely.

"I know, I know," she whispered. "It's okay now. I'm here now."

Even through the stress of the moment, Tess's statement, *I'm here now*, made its way to her inner core. It made Ruth's stomach do a little flip. A flip that she now recognized as attraction and desire. What the hell was happening?

"Come on, let's get a nip. That will calm your nerves."

Chapter Sixteen

Tess led Ruth by the hand to a storage room that was tucked away at the end of a hall. They entered the dark, musty space and Tess closed the door behind them. "We just need a little break from that brute, and any others like him." Tess gingerly sat on the floor, moving a box that was in the way and guided Ruth to the same position beside her.

Ruth had stopped crying and had nearly forgotten the encounter with Rahn. She couldn't believe what was happening to her now.

"Here, got it?" Tess pressed a metal object into Ruth's hand, holding her hand as she did so. "The cap's already off. Don't gulp it, though. It's strong stuff."

If Tess could have seen Ruth's eyes in the little closet, she would have seen them open wide. She could, however, hear Ruth take a large swallow from the little flask and the immediate coughing that followed.

"I told you not to gulp!" Tess scolded. "Hand me that." She took the flask and lifted it to her lips, allowing small sips to enter her mouth at a controlled rate. "Ah, that's the stuff. Here, try again. Slowly this time."

Ruth did as she was told. The English woman was right. Slower was better. She could already feel the heat of the strong liquor make its way down her throat. "Thank you," she said. She realized that they were still holding hands. She didn't let go. She was grateful she hadn't because if she had, she wouldn't have felt the squeeze that Tess gave her.

"My pleasure. Are you sure you're all right?" Tess's heart was still racing from the confrontation with Rahn. Her words had been bold and loud but she knew that a nurse didn't stand a chance against a doctor if charges were brought. She didn't care. She wouldn't let the bully treat a fellow nurse that way. Especially not Ruth.

"I'm fine. You were...very brave."

Tess's face flushed, partly from the liquor and partly from the rush of pleasure that she got at being Ruth's protector, her rescuer.

"I don't know what I would have done if you hadn't shown up when you did."

"Don't worry about that now. I did show up and you're safe now." Another squeeze of the hand.

The women sat in silence. Despite their surroundings, neither intended to leave anytime soon. The physical contact, the warm feeling from the alcohol, and the newfound connection between them was too mesmerizing. They passed the flask back and forth, each limiting themselves to small swallows now, having felt the potency of the drink. It loosened Ruth's tongue enough to ask a question that had been on her mind.

"Why do you cry? At night, I mean? Is it because of the war?"

Tess slid her hand from Ruth's. She hadn't expected the question and was suddenly very aware that she was vulnerable and out of her comfort zone. To her surprise, Ruth took her hand back and squeezed it.

"I'm here now," Ruth said quietly, echoing the

words of comfort that Tess had offered her earlier.

Tess closed her eyes and made a decision. She wanted to talk to this woman; she didn't want the moment to end. But the conversation that Ruth was asking for was so painful. "I don't cry because of the war. I cry because of Rose."

"Your girlfriend? Oh, I'm sorry, Tess." It was the first time Ruth had called her by name and when she did so, she laid a hand gently on the other woman's arm. She could see that her words had hurt Tess and wished instantly that she could take them back. "I understand. I've had my own heart broken, too."

Tess looked at Ruth and smiled wistfully. "It's not what you think. She didn't break my heart, not on purpose, anyway. We were very much in love and then, one day, she was gone."

Ruth was spellbound. "She left you?"

"In a way. She was killed." The words were hard to get out but Tess managed it, without crying this time. But she couldn't stop the tears that sprang to her eyes.

"Oh no," Ruth gasped, her hand going to her mouth involuntarily. "I'm so sorry. That's awful."

Tess swallowed hard. She considered shutting the conversation down, telling the earnest American woman that she just didn't want to talk about it. But, she did. "Fancy a smoke?" Tess asked. She wanted to get out of there.

"Sure."

"The coast should be clear by now and Rahn is likely sleeping it off somewhere. Let's get some air."

Ten minutes later, the women sat together behind the hospital, huddled on a wooden pallet that had most recently held packages of medical supplies for the ward. It was chilly outside, a raw breeze whipping through the area occasionally. Ruth held a cigarette out to Tess, who took it with a grateful nod. It took three tries to light the cigarette with the wind. Tess took a long drag and exhaled as she looked straight ahead.

Ruth was not a frequent smoker, but had picked up the habit since being overseas. It was a social outlet more than anything and she didn't mind the rough feeling it left in the back of her throat. She was silent, sensing that Tess needed to take her time.

"Rose." Tess stopped there. Rose, beautiful Rose. She hadn't spoken of her since it happened. But now, now that she had said her name aloud, there was no going back. "We were at university together. Rose, well, she was much smarter than I am. She was studying literature." Tess's throat tightened as an image of Rose filled her mind. Rose, carrying her books in front of her, in that camel-colored coat that she looked so good in, smiling at Tess.

"Go on," Ruth urged softly.

"Right. She was studying literature and was a very good writer in her own right. Poetry and plays, mostly. Very creative."

Ruth nodded.

"We were friends, good friends, with several classes together. We began taking our lunch at the same time and grew closer. We talked about everything, you know. With Rose...I was able to be more open, more myself." Tess's voice cracked and she paused, willing the emotions to order.

Ruth patted Tess's hand, still not talking, not

wanting to interfere with this sudden floodgate of candor. She had the feeling that if she talked too much, or perhaps even at all, Tess would fall silent.

Tess nodded, a silent acknowledgement of appreciation for Ruth's patience. Then she went on. "Rose was a very good listener, always focused on what we were talking about, interested in me. It was a different experience for me. I hadn't often found a friend who I could trust in that way." She laughed, wryly. "I suppose by hadn't often, I really mean to say never."

The wind continued its onslaught against the women, unforgiving and cold. Neither made any effort to move. Ruth's only acknowledgement of the elements was a quick wipe at her nose, which had begun to run a bit.

"I knew I wasn't like the other girls at university. Wasn't boy crazy. Wasn't really even girl crazy, truth be told. I'd had feelings, in that way, but never acted on them." Tess looked at Ruth, hoping for acceptance. She got it with Ruth's warm eyes and smile upon her. "The more time I spent with her, the more it became apparent that I was Rose-crazy." Tess laughed softly.

Ruth watched carefully as Tess unfolded her story. She was honored that Tess trusted her with her heart's secrets but felt a nagging guilt. Shifting her body on the uncomfortable pallet, she identified the source of the guilt. It was borne of another emotion—jealousy. Hearing Tess speaking so reverentially of Rose, seeing the English woman open up and reveal a sensitive side, Ruth found herself envious of this dead woman whom she would never meet.

Oblivious to Ruth's warring feelings, Tess continued. "I had a sense that Rose was also keen on me, but was terrified to ask her. What if she had said no, you silly bird! I would have died of shame. Even worse, I could have lost her friendship." Tess looked up at Ruth. "I was truly in love with her. I knew that I wanted her in my life no matter how I could get her. If it meant that I could only have her as a friend, I was willing to settle for that. Settle if the alternative meant that I would lose her forever."

Ruth slowly realized as she heard Tess speak that her own feelings for Lillian had never reached those depths. Had she only been playing at love? Mistaking physical pleasure and the freedom of experience with truly being in love?

"And then, one day, it all came to a head."

Tess paused for so long that Ruth couldn't help but ask a question. "What? What happened?"

Closing her eyes briefly, Tess smiled, the memory still powerful despite the time that had passed. "It was quite simple, really. She kissed me." Tess laughed, a sound of pure happiness. She remembered the surprise she had felt when Rose had closed the space between them with one step and, without a second's hesitation, pressed her lips against Tess's. Those soft, full lips, the subject of many of Tess's wistful imaginations, they had been most deliciously and most miraculously joined with Tess's own. The first contact had sent paroxysms of sensations through Tess. Desire, relief, happiness, love. So much emotion that Tess had had to steady herself against Rose, holding her shoulders for support.

Ruth watched the stream of emotions play across Tess's face, her delight in reliving this private memory made no longer private. She found herself smiling at the sight, pleased for Tess. But still, still that pinch of jealousy.

"It was a revelation." Tess looked at Ruth, almost as if she had forgotten she was sitting beside her. She grasped both of Ruth's hands in her own. "You know what that's like, I know you do."

"I do," Ruth said in a near whisper, although she knew as she said it that she wasn't quite sure.

"That kiss changed my life, changed me. I felt as if I had become suddenly a different person. I was happy, free, open. I imagine that's what everyone says when they fall in love."

Ruth's mind had already moved ahead in the narrative. Her heart ached for Tess, to have had this joy only to lose the woman she loved. She had a thousand questions but asked none.

"I was nervous about being intimate with her. I didn't know how and I was afraid I would look foolish." With this admission, Tess looked over at Ruth, almost sheepish.

"That's normal," Ruth said, her wealth of experience with two women under her belt.

"Don't think I didn't want to, though," Tess said with a smile at the memory. "It's all I thought about. So much so that I wondered if something might be wrong with me. I craved her. And she felt the same. We tortured ourselves with hints, suggestions, and kisses."

A tingle between Ruth's legs felt inappropriate. Should she be having feelings of arousal about this woman, this woman who was reliving her life's most awful nightmare?

"And then, finally, the day came. We had met for lunch, a small cafe, our usual spot. It was time for each of us to go back to work and we stood on a street corner." Tess's eyes welled up. "It was always so hard to say good-bye to Rose; I never wanted our moments together to end. She was just about to step off to head her way when I found myself blurting out that I wanted to spend the night with her that night."

The tingles continued for Ruth.

"I felt so brave telling her I wanted to make love, but I did it. It was thrilling. She grabbed my hands and kissed me right there, right in the middle of the street. 'Tonight,' she said." Tess looked out into the distance, remembering the moment only too clearly. "Tonight. She was looking at me when she stepped off, right into the path of a taxi. She never saw it coming."

Tess lost the battle for her emotions and broke down into tears. The sobs were loud, unrestrained. Ruth held her, rocking her gently. "She never saw it coming," Tess repeated when she was able to speak again.

"I'm so sorry," Ruth said into Tess's hair. She was. Despite the jealousy and the tingles, the evident heartache was so immense that Ruth's own heart was hurting.

Tess seemed committed to telling the whole story, a penance of sorts. "It was because of me. If I had just let her go, not said what I said, she would have stepped off of the curb and crossed the street. She wouldn't have been crushed, torn like she was." An ugly-sounding, broken sob tore from her mouth as she saw in her mind's eye the violent accident.

"Oh no, you mustn't blame yourself, Tess." The reason for Tess's sadness and apparent cold demeanor was becoming clear now. "It was an accident. A terrible accident."

Tess shrugged, unconvinced. She wiped her nose and shook her head, as if shaking away the vulnerable side of herself that she had revealed. "Maybe. So, that's my story. Not a happy one. But, for the time that we were together, it was like a dream." She managed a small smile.

The women sat in silence, each lost in their own thoughts. Ruth spoke her realization the moment it hit her. "So, you never made love with Rose. Or with anyone else?" She surprised herself with the boldness of the query.

Tess turned her head sharply and for a moment, was indignant at the question. Just as quickly, she recognized her own automatic defensiveness, the iron guard that she had made for herself to protect from the pain—the pain of losing Rose. She reset herself before answering. "No. Not with anyone."

Ruth's heart broke a little more for Tess. Although not having a wide breadth of sexual experiences with women, the ones she had had were life-changing. She hated that Tess had been deprived of that joy. So far.

"I'm sorry to hear that. I truly am." And she truly was.

Tess nodded. "As am I."

Chapter Seventeen

Ruth had a secret that she hadn't shared with any of the other nurses. She didn't know why she was keeping it private; the women had all grown so close that it seemed a silly thing not to share. Living in close quarters and working elbow to elbow under the roughest conditions had made the women very familial, like sisters in many ways. There was bickering, as one would expect, but under it all, the bonds among the women helped them get through the days, the horrors that they saw daily.

Still, Ruth had a private mission that she kept to herself. Once hoping to travel to all of the states in America, she had changed the goal to helping soldiers from every state. When her patient was able to speak, she would talk to them in recovery or in the ward, ask them about their lives, about where they came from. The young men were only too happy to talk to the pretty young nurse who took an interest in them. Home was so far away and the gentleness of a girl like Ruth was a welcome antidote to the cold, dirty brutality of the war.

Prior to that day in the family room, clustered around the radio, listening to the breathless reports from Pearl Harbor, Ruth had always thought of California as the most exotic place in the world. California, she had thought, must be the most beautiful place on earth, with its Pacific coast, redwoods, big cities, and mountains.

In her mind, Ruth was "collecting" states and she had in fact met numerous young soldiers from California, as well as most of the states (she still needed North Dakota and Vermont).

The game had become less exciting and had grown to a depressing exercise, however. Ruth wasn't sure what she had expected when she started the private endeavor. Maybe the boys from the West would remind her of cowboys that she had read about? The boys from New York would be street-wise and talk with tough accents. The Southern gentlemen would have a pleasant, gentle accent and call her ma'am. Instead, the wartime lesson that Ruth had learned was that no matter which state the boys were from, they were very much the same.

They were young. They were scared. They missed their mothers. They missed their girls. They wanted to be brave but sometimes weren't. They loved their fellow soldiers with a ferocity greater than that reserved for their own brothers. They were proud of what they were doing. Ruth had found these qualities to be universal, no matter if the boy in her ward was from the North, South, East Coast, or West.

There had been the boy from West Virginia, her first "specialed" patient. His legs had been blown off and it was only a matter of time.

"You can special him, dear. We're slow tonight and he's scared," the head nurse on duty had said when Ruth reported on her list of patients.

"Special him?"

The nurse had sighed; her charges were all so young and she was tired. "Special him. It means you can sit with him."

"Sit with him?" Ruth was not following.

The older nurse smiled, a patient smile. This one was an innocent all right. "Sit with him until he dies. You can stay with him and make him comfortable until he passes."

Ruth stared at the nurse. She wasn't sure what struck her the most, the realization that not everyone got the "privilege" of not dying alone or the nurse's calm way of giving her the instructions. In that moment, she realized how sheltered and naïve she was. But that was changing, day by day.

That was how Daniel Satter spent his last hours on the earth. Not in his comfortable and familiar West Virginia deep woods, with his hunting buddies or his numerous brothers, but with a nervous Ruth Carroway, sitting by his side and holding his hand, telling him that it would be okay, when clearly it wouldn't. Daniel Satter was one of the lucky ones. When he stopped breathing, Ruth felt tears spring to her eyes but stopped herself. She couldn't break down; other patients needed her.

There had been the young sailor from Massachusetts, Joseph Maretti. Ruth had delighted in his strong accent and his boisterous personality. Even with his lower body in a cast, Joseph had flirted relentlessly. It was only when the night was quiet and the ward was still when Joseph had let down his tough guy persona.

"Nurse?" he had asked as Ruth checked his vitals during an overnight shift.

"Yes?"

"Can you give me something of yours? Something that smells nice?"

Ruth had given him a skeptical look, which changed immediately when she looked into his dark brown eyes, creased with sadness and a resignation that was devastating to see on a young man. She felt reflexively at the pocket on her uniform. She kept a perfumed handkerchief there, on the sage advice of a nurse who told her it was useful to have to press to her face when burn victims came through.

"Why?" she asked.

Tears welled up in the Italian boy's eyes. "I just don't think I'll ever have a woman close to me again, not with this wrecked body. I just want to smell a woman, that's all."

Ruth nodded, her heart breaking for the boy. She extracted the small handkerchief and held it to Joseph's nose.

He inhaled deeply, his eyes closed. When they opened, he had a smile on his face. "Thank you. You're an angel, ya know that?"

Ruth tucked the handkerchief near the man's neck and smiled, without answering.

And the boy from California, the first one that she had come across, Matthew Polner. He was a good boy, not exotic at all. He had ginger brown hair and freckles that made him look even younger than his nineteen years. He was a brave, good young man. The pile of bloody linens that had been stripped from Matthew Polner's bed after his body was taken away looked no different from the piles that came from the boys from any other state.

≈≈≈≈≈

Dear Mother and Pop,

Thank you for sending the care package. The candies, playing cards, and extra stockings were wonderful. You'll be happy to know that the package went a long way toward making me and a lot of my nursing pals feel like we were home, even if for a short while. We played poker (don't worry, Mother, no gambling) and ate candy and had a grand time.

The friends I have made here are wonderful. I've met nurses from all over the country. There's Midgie from New York, Delilah from Arkansas, Ruby from Texas, and Shorty from California. (By the way, we call her Shorty because she is almost six feet tall, as tall as Frank!). I've also met nurses from France and of course, England. The interesting thing is that even though we are from all over the country (and world), we all seem to have so much in common.

How are you doing at home? Do you get much news from the front? Try not to worry; the Carroway kids are safe and sound.

Love,
Ruth

Chapter Eighteen

D^{ear Sis,}

I sure was surprised to hear that you're over here, too! I don't know when you'll get this letter, seems like the mail takes a very long time to get to where it's supposed to go. I got two of your letters; as you probably know now, mail call is a real highlight so keep those letters coming.
It seems like I've been here for a lifetime! Our platoon has seen a lot of action and we move around a lot. My platoon mates are great guys. It's hard to imagine that I've only known some of them for a few months. They feel like brothers. It's strange that guys I've only just met are closer to me than any of the fellows I went to high school with. I feel like I understand Dad a bit better, having seen some of the things I've seen. I can see why he didn't want to talk about it much. When we get home, we can share some stories! Who would have thought that the two Carroways would end up at war together?
I better close here. I'm almost out of space on this piece of paper. Take good care of yourself, little sister. And watch out for those

GIs! Don't let them sweet talk you.

Your brother,
Frank

❧❧❧❧

The nurses had decided to throw an impromptu party. Someone had gotten a half bottle of whiskey and that, along with a well-worn big band album, was all that they needed for a welcome reprieve from their duties.

"Let's move all of this and make a dance floor," Betty suggested. The women agreed readily and set to work pushing the tables and chairs from the center of the social room. It was hardly a dance floor, but again, this was hardly a party. Everything was relative when you were at war.

Someone put the album on the phonograph and the room was instantly transformed. Music was the universal antidote to doldrums and despair and nowhere was it needed more than wartime London. Several of the nurses clapped with happiness automatically when they heard the first strains of Miller's tunes.

"Pass it around," Midgie said after she had taken a generous swig from the whiskey bottle. She opened her eyes wide for comic effect and patted her chest. "That'll put some hair on your chest, girls." She passed the bottle to Ruth.

Ruth took a swallow, not on the level of Midgie's gulp, but still, a generous amount of the fiery liquid. "Oh my goodness!" she said, once she could talk again. The heat of the liquor coursed its way through her and she felt every bit of movement.

The women continued laughing and talking, all of them dancing and drinking. If not for the setting, of course, one would have thought they had stepped into a Saturday night social in the States. Each woman felt a weight lifted as she let go of the stress of their world, even if just for an evening. They needed this.

One woman who wasn't dancing, or drinking for that matter, was Tess. Tess sat in a corner, reading a book, quiet as usual. But Ruth saw the smile in Tess's eyes as she listened to the music. Her foot was tapping and Ruth could have sworn that she saw Tess sway a bit in her chair. The stern visage evaporated and Ruth saw the real Tess, the one who must have existed before Rose left. Afraid to look for too long, knowing that if Tess saw that she was being watched the shell would return, Ruth continued dancing.

It felt so good to be free from the horror of the war, the grim bloodiness of the OR, the nagging homesickness. Who would have guessed that something as simple as music could have provided such a joyous reprieve? Ruth absorbed the happiness of her fellow nurses, all dancing and laughing, holding hands with one another as they enjoyed the sounds of Glenn Miller. She stole another glance at Tess. Again, she was rewarded with a peek at the Tess that was kept hidden. It was a thrill to see her eyes shine and the small smile threatening the corners of her mouth. *That must be the Tess that Rose knew*, Ruth thought.

Inspired, Ruth glided over to Tess's chair.

"Dance with us!" she said, extending a hand.

The moment Ruth approached, the armor returned. Ruth watched the change overtake Tess's face, almost as if by magic trick—now you see me, now you don't.

"No, thank you." Tess said politely, looking down at her book.

Disappointment washed over Ruth. She regretted her impulsive move immediately. Not only did Tess not want to join in, Ruth's intrusion had sent her back inside of herself.

"You sure?" Ruth asked.

Tess raised her book, *How Green Was My Valley*. "I've got my novel."

Ruth nodded and backed away. She returned to the group of dancing nurses but the exhilaration was muted.

Chapter Nineteen

Dear Daughter,

We hope this letter finds you safe and well. Your father and I miss you terribly and think about you always. The house is so empty and quiet without you and your brother.

Dad's garden is still the best on the block and of course, he is as proud as ever. I'm continuing my work with the war mothers and find that it helps to pass the time and keep my mind occupied.

We are sending a package to you with things we think you might be missing. Please write and tell us what you need and if we can get our hands on it, we'll be sure to send it right away.

How are your duties? It's hard to imagine you as a nurse but we know you're doing a fine job. Are you meeting lots of nice nurses? You've always been so good at making friends, I am sure they surround you over there.

Please be safe and know that you are in our prayers always. We are both very proud of you, Ruth.

Love,
Mother

The next morning, Ruth woke up in stages. She had the sensation of being pulled up through layers of concrete, each one thinner than the last until finally, she was awake. Her head was pounding from the previous night's liquor and she felt awful. She looked around the bunkroom. It was still very early morning and the room was quiet, unusually so. Many of the bunks were occupied, tired nurses sleeping hard after playing hard. Some were empty; those would be the night shift nurses. The empty beds were neatly made, an unspoken courtesy by the women. It could be difficult living in such close quarters, with little space and less privacy, but keeping your area neat and tidy was easy enough and appreciated by everyone.

She turned over in her bed, relishing the silence, and stretched out. The bed beside her, Tess's, was empty, with Tess apparently already on duty. A little smile found its way to Ruth's still tired face as she thought of Tess efficiently making her bed, tucking in the corners as if her life depended on it. Ruth had watched the procedure numerous times and thought it amusing that, in the midst of all of this chaos, Tess put such effort and pride in something as ordinary as making her bunk. Tess always turned back for a final look at the bed before she left the room, as if to make sure it looked ship-shape from all angles.

The rest of Tess's small area revealed little about the woman. The small bedside table held a single picture of an older man and woman, Tess's parents presumably. Unlike many of the others, Tess didn't keep any memorabilia or reminders of loved ones on her table. It was all business. Just like Tess. Ruth wondered if somewhere in Tess's things there was a photo of Rose, hidden away like Tess's pain.

※※※※

"How'd this kid get in here?" The surgeon had been up for twenty-fours straight and operating through most of that time. He was exhausted and had no patience for the intrusion. Besides, the damn kid reminded him of his own small son at home and that was something he couldn't deal with, not when he was over here and not when he was in the middle of a surgery that likely wouldn't save his patient's life.

"Sorry, Doctor," Ruth said. She glared at the boy over her mask and jerked her head toward the door. "Go, Gabriel."

The young boy scampered off. Despite her fierce countenance, Gabriel knew that Ruth wasn't angry with him. She smiled underneath her mask, thinking about the chocolate and hard-boiled eggs that she had held for him. She knew he would return to the nurse's quarters that evening, around dinnertime, to see if any of the women had anything for him.

"We should turn him in," Delilah had said. She was a nurse from Arkansas, very much by the book. "His parents are probably looking for him."

"Delilah, open your eyes. His parents are dead. That's why he's coming around. Poor kid doesn't have anyone but us," Lorna chided. She had a big heart, this New York girl from a huge family. She always saved something for the boy, her soul hurting at the thought of him growing up alone when she had been blessed with such a big, wonderful family.

"Still. The authorities should know. They would

take him somewhere." Delilah wasn't giving up.

"I hate to tell you, sweetie, but rounding up orphans isn't tops on the priority list these days," another nurse chimed in.

"All right, you hens," the surgeon scolded. "Enough. Deal with your hard-luck cases later. For now, we're trying to save this kid."

※※※※

The OR had been particularly gruesome. A platoon had been firebombed and the hospital saw a rash of burn victims, some so badly burned that they were barely recognizable as human. Ruth had to sniff her perfumed handkerchief several times to keep from being sick. She could see in the other nurses' eyes over their masks that they were struggling, too. She remembered hearing the Pearl Harbor reports, how horrified she had been at the images she imagined from the burning U.S.S. Arizona. The things she had seen since then, including today, were far, far worse than anything she had ever imagined.

※※※※

That night, Ruth fingered the hard candies in the pocket of her uniform as she stood outside of the hospital. The street was a jumble of concrete and building rubble but enough had been cleared away to allow for some semblance of movement and activity. Few people were out, however, as there could always be a bombing. Still, Ruth craved fresh air and a respite from the hospital. She closed her eyes against the weak sunlight and imagined she was back home, lying on a hammock in the back yard, with a glass of lemonade in her hand and not a care in the world. If she had felt like a teenager when she left America, she certainly felt like an adult now, and she was aware on some level that she had missed a step somewhere in between. The brutality of war, the pace of her days, the things she had seen... each had made Ruth a different person. She couldn't decide if it had made her a better person, but certainly a different one.

She knew that Gabriel would be making his rounds soon and hoped to see him. Seeing the boy always raised her spirits, even if she had to force herself not to think of his orphaned state. After a day like today's in the OR, she needed a lift. In addition to the candies, which she had saved from a package from home, Ruth had another surprise for Gabriel.

Fifteen minutes later, Ruth broke into a wide smile when she saw the slight child turn the corner. When he saw his favorite nurse, Gabriel too grinned and began to run toward her.

"Wait!" Ruth called out.

Gabriel stopped short, confused. Even children learned that when your city is a warzone, any admonition to wait or not move was to be taken seriously.

"Hold on," Ruth said. She reached into her pocket and extracted a small ball, another prize from home, sent at her request for this exact purpose. "Can you catch?"

Gabriel's body untensed and he laughed aloud. "Very well, thank you. Give me a toss!"

Ruth performed an exaggerated wind-up and sailed the ball toward the boy, who caught it neatly with one hand. He threw it back, using a gentle underhand. The ball fell short.

"Don't take it easy on me!" Ruth said as she moved to pick up the ball. She threw it back and crouched into a catcher's stance.

"All right then!" Gabriel threw the ball hard and accurately. When Ruth caught it cleanly, he cheered.

The two played catch for nearly half an hour, ignoring their bleak surroundings and what the rest of the day held for them. For that brief moment in time, it was just a boy and a young woman laughing, bragging, and playing.

"This was the best day in a long time," Gabriel said, giving Ruth a shy hug after they ended their game.

"Yes, it was," Ruth said, resting her chin on top of the boy's head. "Yes, it was."

Chapter Twenty

"Anyone who's available needs to fall in for a field run," Midgie yelled from the doorway of the bunkroom.

The nurses started moving immediately. "What's happened, Midgie?" Ruby asked.

"Another bombing. One of the neighborhoods is a terrible wreck. They want us to canvas the area for survivors and tend to the civilians." Midgie looked grave, which was unusual for her personality. "Better hurry," she said before rushing off.

Ruth had one thought…Gabriel. Something in her heart told her she had to find Gabriel. She pulled on her uniform and raced out of the room, not waiting for the others.

※ ※ ※ ※

Midgie had been right; the neighborhood was a disaster zone. Ruth coughed, trying to clear the hot dust from her lungs. What once had been a delightful little area, full of thriving shops and cozy homes, was now nearly unrecognizable.

Ruth carefully stepped around piles of rubble. She saw a woman's severed arm in pile, a shredded tatter of flowered cloth still on it. The body that it had been connected to was nowhere in sight. She forced herself to continue. She had to find Gabriel. She would help look for other survivors later.

"Ma'am!" a voice called out.

Ruth looked to see a young English soldier kneeling over a body. She couldn't tell if the body was dead or alive. Or if it was an adult or child. She rushed over.

"You're a nurse; please help my friend," the soldier said. His voice and barely there facial stubble revealed his youth. His own condition looked grave—one arm hung uselessly to his side and ominous dark blood was dripping from his nose.

His friend looked even worse and Ruth was sure that he would be dead within the hour. A massive head wound was the most obvious injury and only the bloody street held his brain inside of his cracked skull. His eyes were closed and a grimace was what would be his final expression. Ruth caressed the man's forehead. "Poor soul," she whispered.

"Can you help him?" his friend asked. His eyes were wide and scared and Ruth could see that he trusted her.

Ruth wondered if blind hope or shock made the friend believe that the man lying on the road could be saved. She couldn't lie to the man and she didn't have time to linger. Gabriel was out there somewhere.

"I'm sorry, but he is too seriously injured to be saved. He is going to die. You need to stay here until help can come for you." She patted the soldier's hand and left him without another word. She didn't look back; she couldn't. She knew if she turned around to see the young man's face, she might have stayed and she simply couldn't do that. She had to find Gabriel; after all, he was just a boy and he was alone.

The city was a disaster zone and not for the first

time Ruth wondered if the people back home in the United States had any idea what it was like in Europe. She wondered if it was possible to convey the horror in a letter home or a news article. *No*, she decided. *It is not.* She knew that for herself, if she wasn't seeing the sights for herself, with her own eyes, she never would have believed that men could be so cruel to one another as to destroy towns and people with such mercenary resolve.

Ruth continued to search, looking at every pile of rubble and calling Gabriel's name. Thirty minutes after leaving the English soldier and his doomed friend, she encountered a medical party. After giving directions to the soldier's location, Ruth felt a lightness and sense of happiness for a moment, a small sliver of hope. It was enough to give her strength to keep going. She hoped that the young soldier would be saved, even if his friend would not. So many boys would not be going home; she wanted desperately to think that she had helped at least that one on his way.

It was in that moment that Ruth looked up and saw a sight that brought instant tears to her eyes. Gabriel was one hundred yards in front of her. She blinked, wondering if exhaustion and emotion were making her eyes play tricks on her. He was still there. He was climbing on a pile of rubble, trying to get into a bakery storefront. His clothes were dirty but there he was, alive and well.

"Gabriel!" Ruth shouted joyfully.

Gabriel leaned backward from the pile at the sound of his name and spotted Ruth. A bright smile emerged and he waved. The boy climbed atop the pile and grabbed a partially destroyed ledge to pull himself up to an upper level balcony apartment above the bakery. "Look at me! I've found some bread!"

Ruth hurried toward the bakery. Her heart soared at the sight of Gabriel and his beautiful smile. "Good boy," she yelled through a cupped hand. *Leave it to Gabriel to find something good in a disaster like this*, she thought.

At that moment, the balcony ledge upon which Gabriel was standing crumbled, sending him plummeting to the pile of rubble below. He let loose a short yelp right before the third level of the side of the building, weakened by the loss of its supporting level, slid down and buried him in a pile of rock and debris. The heavy building material sheeting down the wall made a horrific and sickening sound. Ruth had no way of knowing that the sound she had just heard was one that would play out in her mind for years and years to come.

Ruth froze, horrified. A small puff of rock dust floated up from the pile. Gabriel was nowhere to be seen. "Oh my God!" Ruth cried. Her legs refused to move.

Two American soldiers in uniform patrolling the area rushed toward the bakery from the other direction. They pawed frantically at the rubble, throwing pieces to the side as they dug. Their hands quickly became bloodied as the rough edges were ignored and grabbed. The men's faces held a grim determination as if they couldn't bear to see another casualty this day. Still, Ruth could not move. Abruptly, the men stopped. They looked at each other and sagged.

Finally, Ruth found her legs. She covered the distance to the bakery, screaming Gabriel's name. Before she could get to the pile, one of the men met her and blocked her access.

"No, lady. Don't come any closer."

"Gabriel! I need to see him."

"I'm sorry. He's gone."

Ruth stared at the man. She looked at his dirty, dusty face and sad eyes and knew that she would never forget what he looked like as long as she lived. "No."

"I'm sorry."

"Just let me see him," she said, trying to push past the man.

He grabbed her by the shoulders. "No. You don't want to do that."

Ruth was angry now. The anger felt better than the alternative. "I'm a nurse, for God's sakes. I've seen death."

"You haven't seen this."

Ruth looked again at the sad eyes. She knew he was right. "Did he suffer?" she asked. It was a silly question. The soldier had no idea.

But this soldier was a kind man. What he had seen under the debris would haunt him for the rest of his life, more than anything else he would see during the war. He gave Ruth a gift. "He didn't feel anything at all. He didn't suffer. I promise."

Ruth nodded, forcing herself not to cry. "Thank you." With that, she turned around on one heel and walked all of the way back to the barracks.

※※※※

Ruth ignored the greetings of several nurses and a doctor as she made her way through the hospital and toward the bunkroom. She didn't want to see anybody; she didn't want to talk to anybody. She just wanted to lie down and close her eyes. She prayed that when she closed her eyes, she would be able to shut down the part of her brain that was creating fearsome images of what young Gabriel's body must have looked like under that rubble.

The bunkroom was nearly empty, with a couple of nurses sitting on a bed, playing cards and talking quietly. Ruth headed toward her bunk and frowned when she saw it was stripped down to the old, worn mattress. She had taken all of her bedding and washed it and it now was drying in the laundry area. She sat on the edge of the bed, feeling adrift.

Poor Gabriel, poor sweet boy, she thought. She pictured his face and bright smile, the warm eyes that held such hope despite being in such a hopeless place. She wondered if she could have taken him home with her to Indiana. It was silly, she knew. But what if? She could see him riding his bicycle with other boys along the streets, a baseball card attached in his spokes. It was what a boy his age should be doing, not scavenging for bread in a warzone with no parents to go home to.

The unfairness of the war washed over Ruth. The anger came quickly and galvanized her. She couldn't go through this again. Why had she let herself become attached to the boy? He was just a boy, a stranger. She vowed not to let herself expose her heart to such pain again. She was here to do a job, that's what she would do.

"You okay?"

Ruth looked up to see Tess peering at her, her face revealing concern. She realized that her own face had tightened with determination and anger, prompting Tess's inquiry.

"Fine, thank you."

Tess sat on her own bed and looked at Ruth. "You

don't look fine. Someone said you had gone out after the bombing, to look for the boy. Did you find him?"

The resolve flickered inside of Ruth. She wanted to be comforted but knew Tess wouldn't be the one to do it. It wasn't her style. Besides, the time to harden herself, to toughen up started now. "He was killed."

Tess's hand went to her mouth. "The boy?"

Ruth nodded, afraid her voice might not be able to keep up with her newfound stoicism.

"Oh my God," Tess exclaimed. Her eyes watered. "He was just a boy." She looked at Ruth with new eyes. "Are you okay? I know the two of you were...close."

Ruth was ready to proclaim her invincibility but made the mistake of looking at Tess. The tears in Tess's eyes and quiet concern in her voice pierced Ruth. She felt her throat tighten painfully and then the tears began to slice down her cheeks, their hotness a betrayal of the attempt to shut out the pain.

"No, no, you're not, are you," Tess said, more to herself than to Ruth.

"It's not fair!" Ruth cried. Once those words came out, Ruth felt herself crumble internally. She felt the pain everywhere, in her heavy heart, the pit of her stomach, and the emptiness all around her.

To Ruth's complete shock, Tess held up her open arms. She didn't say a word, just beckoned Ruth to come over, offering her some strength.

Ruth stared at Tess for a moment before propelling herself in the open arms. It was exactly what she needed.

Tess wrapped her arms around the sobbing woman and guided her to the bed. She held her as she cried and stroked her hair gently, occasionally murmuring comforting words to Ruth.

Ruth was so upset about Gabriel that it took her several minutes to realize what was happening. Tess was showing a side of herself that Ruth wasn't sure existed. The tenderness with which she held Ruth, the sweet tone that she was using as she spoke to her, all of these were new to Ruth. In a place below the raw grief Ruth was feeling, she knew something else was growing. She held tight to Tess, finding solace in her arms and a flicker of hope.

An hour later, Ruth felt she was cried out. Her face and eyes were swollen from her tears and her head hurt. She sat up slowly and wiped her nose. She was sure she looked a mess.

Tess offered her a smile. "Better?"

Ruth nodded. "A little." She looked at the rumpled bed, usually so tidy and neat. "I messed up your bunk," Ruth said, her voice congested from crying.

"I noticed. I imagine I'll forgive you this once." Tess winked and again, Ruth felt that nascent glimmer of something special.

Chapter Twenty-one

The days following Gabriel's death were difficult. Ruth couldn't let go of the unfairness, the injustice of war taking a boy so young. She was also feeling a deep sense of regret. If only she had done more for the boy, perhaps tried to find a home for him or even talked the senior staff into allowing him to stay with the nurses, perhaps he would be alive. What might he have grown into, that sweet fellow? Ruth's heart hurt at the experiences Gabriel would never have. He would never finish school, never fall in love, never marry, never have an occupation, never have children. It was all such a waste. Having seen up close the stolen lives of so many young men who would never make it home, the too early demise of an innocent child hit Ruth hard.

In bed after a long shift, Ruth pondered her own situation. She hadn't been a child when she came here but in many ways, she had felt like one. Worried about what her parents would think of her every move, feeling like second fiddle to Frank, and not quite owning who she was. Things were different now. She had matured in many ways, some that she wasn't even fully aware of yet. One gift that she had gained from her time overseas was that of introspection. With it came a cost, however. Deep personal insight reveals things that one may not want to deal with or even acknowledge. It calls for action and is the enemy of inaction.

Night wore on and the bunkroom was silent save for the quiet snores of some of the women. The room was dark but beginning to glow just the slightest bit with the morning sun emerging. It would be daylight soon. What would the new day bring for Ruth? She knew it was within her power to guide her own days, at least in part. Certainly, there were aspects of life that were uncontrollable, but there were also opportunities to create one's own destiny. What would a fifty-year old Ruth say to the one lying in the early dawn, sleepless, so very far from home? Ruth realized that the one thing she would hate the most was the thing that had the power to eat through your soul, to travel with you for a lifetime with no respite: regret.

Exhausted in body but buoyed in spirit, Ruth resolved to eliminate any regrets that she might be creating the groundwork for. She was growing up, in more ways than one.

※ ※ ※ ※

Ruth fidgeted at the bar, wishing her beer were colder, but mostly wishing she was somewhere else. She had asked Helene to meet her for a drink. "I have something to talk to you about," Ruth had said. Helene, in a rush to get to the ward, had told her to be at the bar at seven.

It was 7:15 p.m. now and Helene was nowhere in sight. Ruth sighed, irritated at the delay. *She thinks she can do whatever she likes, no matter about wasting someone else's time*, Ruth thought. Not that she had anything in particular to do at the moment. But still, it was the principle. Helene could make Ruth feel like an inferior little sister, insignificant, an afterthought.

Leaving her waiting at the bar was simply more of the same.

At half past the hour, Helene strode in. Even in her aggravated state, Ruth couldn't help but stare, nor could numerous men in the bar. Helene always made an entrance, even in a makeshift dive bar. She wore a sweater that accentuated her full bosom and those long legs got her to the bar in short order.

"Ruth, my sweet. There you are." Helene squeezed Ruth's hand and didn't notice or didn't care that Ruth didn't squeeze back.

"I've been here for half an hour. You're late," Ruth said.

"*Je suis désolée*," Helene said, holding her hands over her heart.

"I assume that means you're sorry."

Helene laughed, a lilting sound that was as beautiful as she was. "It does. Do you forgive me?"

Ruth shook her head, trying not to let the sweater distract her. "I have something to talk to you about. Something important."

"What is it, cherie? What is so serious? You are not going to tell me that I have made you pregnant are you?" Helene laughed at her own joke.

"We can't be together anymore."

Helene frowned, her laugh stopped short. "What do you mean?"

"We can't be...intimate anymore."

"Why ever not?" Helene asked, her eyebrows indicating confusion.

"Well, I have feelings for someone else now. That's why." Ruth didn't feel as satisfied as she had envisioned when she had practiced making this speech.

Helene laughed again. "Don't be silly. That is of

no matter. Of course we can still be intimate."

Ruth's eyes widened. "No, Helene. I don't want that."

"You're being childish. Who is this other person?"

Ruth responded instantly, even though she realized a moment later that she could have simply told the French woman that it was none of her business. "Tess. Tess Davies."

Helene leaned back in her chair and regarded Ruth. "The English girl? You're not serious."

"I am serious. I'm sorry."

Helene moved her chair back and stood up. "Sorry? For what? You were an interesting diversion, that is all. Enjoy your cold fish. I suspect you'll be back." Without so much as a good-bye, Helene was gone.

Ruth watched the back of her former lover retreat and came to a startling conclusion. Helene's feelings were hurt. As much as part of her wanted to be glad that she had made an impact on Helene, part of her felt badly as well. Had she made the right decision?

※ ※ ※ ※

Ruth's plan of taking charge of her life and seizing the day had a second phase after telling Helene. Now, she would tell Tess how she felt. She knew she was taking a chance but she couldn't let herself take the easy way out, the path of least resistance. Doing that had made most of her life empty, kept her from being her true self. *No longer*, Ruth told herself.

The bunkroom was only half full as evening fell, with many of the nurses still on duty from a particularly heavy influx of casualties. Helene had apparently gone elsewhere, likely straight to Margo, and was nowhere to be seen. Ruth was thankful for her absence. She carefully circled her bed with sheets on the clotheslines above it, creating a tent-like private space. Ruth could feel Tess watching her from the next bunk over, although she tried to appear engrossed in a book. When her preparations were complete, Ruth stood at Tess's bedside.

"Join me?" Ruth asked quietly.

Tess looked up and Ruth could tell that her instinct was to say no. Before she could speak, Ruth added a simple entreaty.

"Please." It was one word, but it conveyed so much. Please take a chance. Please trust me. Please let down that wall.

Tess opened her mouth to decline but Ruth's eyes locked with hers. The earnest, open eyes of the American took the words from Tess's mouth and to Ruth's surprise, Tess stood up, placed her book on her own bunk, and stepped through the sheet to Ruth's bed.

Ruth couldn't stop herself from smiling as she followed Tess and climbed on the bunk, pulling the sheets shut behind her. Her heart was racing and she reminded herself to breathe.

The women sat facing one another. Pleasant anticipation filled the small space.

"You know what this is about," Ruth said. She was prepared to make her case, to plead her feelings for Tess and tell her that she had slowly fallen in love with her. She was prepared to open her heart and take a chance, because the chance to be with Tess was worth it. But she didn't have to say a word.

"I can't bear to be hurt again. Not like before…

with Rose." Tess's tone was hesitant. "I just can't."

Ruth felt a flush of relief: Tess hadn't rejected her outright. Even better, Tess had known what was coming. Did that mean she felt the same way? But Ruth knew she couldn't compete with the memory of a dead lover. Worse, Rose had left Tess scarred, hardened, and with her guard permanently up. How could Ruth get through the walls?

"Tess, please. Believe in me. I'm not going anywhere. Please give us a chance." Ruth wished that she had more words, more ways to convey to Tess what she was feeling. There was so much in her heart, if only she could impress upon Tess how much she cared. She knew that Tess's experience with Rose had been not only traumatic but also formative.

Tess buried her face in Ruth's chest. Her heart and head warred with one another. A hard heart would protect Tess from hurt, this much she knew. But at what cost? She too had been dealing with regret, a regret so painful that it had nearly taken over her existence. She did the best she could. "Let's just hold each other tonight. Would that be okay?"

Ruth smiled. It was more than okay with her. The thought of holding this marvelous woman throughout the night was thrilling and more importantly, it was a start.

They situated themselves side by side and without preface, Tess kissed Ruth. It was a gentle, tender kiss and it melted Ruth. She thought back to their discussion, about a kiss being a revelation. It was exactly what it was. Yes, it was definitely a start.

Tess smiled before turning her back to Ruth as she lay on one side. Ruth slid in close to Tess, her hand falling naturally to Tess's bare hip, which her nightshirt pushing up had exposed.

The women sighed in unison and settled in.

"This is nice," Tess said.

"Very."

"I never had the chance to...do this with Rose. I'm sorry; I don't mean to bring her up."

"It's okay," Ruth said softly. "I understand." She did. She had already had her firsts and she knew what a powerful experience this was for Tess. She didn't let Tess's mention of her former love affect her. She didn't begrudge Tess the memory but was ready to make new ones with her.

Ruth thrilled with the touch of Tess's smooth fullness, the pure femininity of the curves. Tucking her own waist in tightly behind Tess's rear, Ruth's eyes closed with an uneasy mix of desire and contentment. Was she being unfair, promising Tess that she would always be there?

Ruth's mind drifted from thoughts of emotions and went into automatic. The warmth of Tess's body against her thighs was anything but relaxing. Ruth could feel her body reacting. Ten minutes later, Ruth's body made a decision for her. This wasn't going to be a quiet night of cuddling. If Tess turned her away, she would of course respect her decision. But if Tess was feeling anything like Ruth was...

Sliding one hand across Tess's naked rear, Ruth felt Tess pull her outer leg up, opening her legs. She heard the soft sound of wetness and knew in an excited instant that Tess was aroused. Moving her arm up, Ruth cupped Tess's heavy breast under her nightshirt, boldly squeezing her. When she felt Tess push her butt into her lap, Ruth groaned, an involuntary reaction to their bodies sliding into a primal position.

Tess leaned her head back in a haze of arousal. She felt Ruth nuzzle the back of her neck while tightening her hand on Tess's breast. Tess reached behind her back until she felt Ruth's bottom and pushed into her, meeting the movement with a movement of her own. Her sleepiness burned away in a flash of desire, Tess put her hand on top of Ruth's, increasing the pressure on her breast, which responded automatically.

"Ruth," she murmured. Tess moved her outer leg higher and moaned softly when she felt Ruth slip a hand between her legs.

Aware of their semi-public surroundings, they struggled to remain quiet. Their bodies had other ideas.

Ruth's breathing quickened when she felt Tess's wetness under her hand and she felt a surge of primitive sexual power. *I did that*, she thought. *I made this beautiful woman want me.* The thought, practically just an internal whisper, sent Ruth's body into overdrive. She pulled her fingers down and through Tess's sex and was rewarded with Tess's blossoming in her hand, felt her opening underneath her. She pushed a finger inside of Tess, then two, and heard the Englishwoman gasp with pleasure. Tess's hand tightened on Ruth's, still pinning Tess's breast.

Ruth started to push into Tess, delighting in the contact against her swollen center. The women were moving together now, without words or instruction, their bodies and pure, perfect desire leading them.

"Yes, my love," Tess murmured. "Yes." She adjusted her legs, allowing Ruth room to penetrate her even more deeply and cried out when Ruth quickly did so.

"Too much?" Ruth asked in her ear, her words breathless but concerned.

"No. Please, keep going."

Ruth pumped in and out of her partner, reveling in the ability to give Tess such pleasure. Ruth's own pleasure was nearing its peak as she slammed again and again into Tess. She felt a wave of hot pleasure flood her face and then drift down her entire body before it pulsed out from her center in near-violent spasms of delight.

A moment later, Tess arched her back and cried out, a wordless sound of release and joy. She felt a warmth flood from her and onto Ruth's fingers and gasped for air.

When the two were spent, still breathing heavily and Ruth still inside of her lover, Tess giggled. Ruth couldn't believe the sound. The gentle happiness of it made her heart swell and she told herself she would never forget this moment, never forget the perfectness of being with this woman.

"I'm sorry," Tess apologized immediately. "I don't know why on earth I'm laughing. That was just so, so...delightful."

Now Ruth was laughing. "Delightful? You make it sound like an afternoon tea!"

The women continued to laugh, happy and scoured clean with the relief of ecstasy. Tess turned so that they faced one another.

"Much better than any tea, love."

Chapter Twenty-two

It had started a normal day, if there was such a thing during wartime. Ruth had gotten up early to allow herself enough time to do some laundry. After a quick breakfast in the mess hall, the usual powdered eggs and toast, Ruth had reported early for her shift. Her motive wasn't entirely one motivated by a strong ethic. Tess had been on the late night shift in the ward and as a senior nurse, her shift bled into the morning shift by one hour to ensure a smooth and effective transition between the nurses. By reporting early, Ruth would be able to share at least the same space with Tess for just a bit longer. The last few weeks had been blissful. With stolen moments together, passionate encounters and always professions of love, the two women had found happiness that neither had ever thought possible.

With one last tuck of her hair under her nursing cap, Ruth took a deep breath before pushing through the swinging doors that led to the ward. Despite the excitement of seeing her lover, Ruth still needed to get her mindset in place every time that she went on duty. The work was physically demanding, with no allowance made for being a woman, but more than that, it was emotionally taxing. Ruth couldn't remember a single day that she had spent on the ward where she had not seen a soldier die. No matter how skilled the doctors were, no matter how skilled the nurses were, it seemed that the Axis combatants were equally skilled at killing the young boys that flowed through the ward. And they were so young, so terribly young.

The ward was quiet, still dimmed for the night, in the hopes that some of the patients would be able to sleep, despite their pain, suffering, and fear. As the room woke up, the patients began to stir. The nurses on the night shift looked exhausted. The body wasn't meant to be up all night, but that was exactly what the women did, tirelessly.

Tess had been watching the standard issue twenty-four-hour clock tick away the hours, not so much to urge her shift to a close but to urge Ruth's shift to a start. She had hoped that Ruth would come in before her report time but had warned herself not to be disappointed if she didn't. *She's tired, too*, Tess had thought, prepping herself. Even the hour that their shifts were sure to overlap was a welcome one. Since they had become lovers, Tess had found herself filled with such a longing for Ruth. It was more than physical, although the treasured moments they spent in one another's arms were certainly a draw. Ruth's presence was such a comfort, a place of safety and warmth and… love. Tess had been hesitant to allow herself to think in those terms. She didn't want to be hurt again. But her connection with Ruth was undeniable.

Suddenly, Ruth was there. Tess sensed her presence before she saw her and looked up from the patient chart in her hands to see Ruth look at her from across the room. A tingle of anticipation and excitement made its way through the English woman and she found that she had been holding her emotional breath, waiting for the young American's appearance. And now, now she was here.

When their eyes met, the sterile, depressing ward shrank away to nothingness. It was just the two of them, each feeling that familiar lightness upon seeing the other. The shared look was intimate, despite the distance and despite the setting. Neither knew it about the other, of course, but each was seeing the other in her mind's eye, not in nurse's garb and not here, but nude, in bed. The newness of their relationship, as well as the newness of lovemaking in general, had kept them both in a semi-permanent state of slow arousal, ready for the slightest look to trigger it, the slightest touch of the other.

"Carroway," Tess said by way of greeting as Ruth made her way closer.

"Nurse Davies," Ruth responded, with a sly smile.

The women's attraction to one another was painted on their faces, obvious to any who might have been paying attention. But no one was. Instead, the patients' attention was on their own recovery, the status of their comrades in arms, or their girls left back home. The other nurses were too tired to care. And the doctors...the doctors were absorbed in their own endless task, the stitching up of young men, the sometimes futile effort to save lives that had barely begun. Ironically, in this most dangerous of places, an active war zone, the only thing that had become safer was a refuge for women like Ruth and Tess. No one had the energy or time to nose into their business, to make trouble, or openly judge. Here, the concern was survival. If two women had fallen in love and were taking pleasure in one another, all the better. Each person at the hospital would rather have been somewhere else. As a result, they kept their heads down and focused on their business, hoping for the war to end.

Ruth stood close to Tess. The patient that Tess had been caring for was sound asleep, aided by the powerful morphine that likely would become an addiction if he lived long enough. But that was a big if. "You look tired, my love," Ruth said softly.

It was true. Tess's hair was tousled and in disarray as a result of assisting with lifting a young man from his operating gurney to a recovery bed. He had been panicky as he emerged from sedation, his hands flying, striking Tess in the face and grabbing her hair. The soldier, a boy really, had died two hours later. Dark smudges of fatigue dominated her face, making her eyes less bright than usual. Blood splatters were on her otherwise spotless uniform. Just another day.

Ruth's use of the endearment "my love" revived Tess's spirit, if not her exhausted body. Her relationship with Rose had never blossomed to this level so all of the adornments of open love were new to Tess and very welcome.

"I'll see you after your shift then?" Tess asked, her question lilting hopefully at the end.

"Yes, I'd like that," Ruth said. She had to hold her hands to her side to prevent herself from reaching for Tess. She wanted nothing more than to hold Tess close to her, to stroke her hair, to ease her fatigue, and make her feel good. But this was not the time, or place. The promise of their time together later allowed Ruth to push through the stark longing, the physical need to touch Tess.

Tess sensed what was going through Ruth's mind. The same thoughts were going through hers as well. Her eyes actually closed for an instant, the pangs of need so powerful that she needed to close herself off briefly. When she opened her eyes, Ruth was still there.

That was when Tess realized something powerful. Ruth was still there. She was here, with Tess. Their attraction had gone beyond flirtation and suggestion. They were lovers. The reality of it struck Tess with an intense force, so much so that she felt weak. "Until later, then, my love," Tess said softly, her eyes on Ruth's.

The promise of those words, so simple yet so telling, was not lost on Ruth. Her smile was broad and obvious. She loved this woman. And, it seemed, Tess was feeling the same.

Before they could exchange any more words, Betty came into the nursing ward and took a quick look around the room before laying eyes on Ruth. As soon as she saw her, her mouth moved in an unmistakable expression of regret, sadness, and dread, all wrapped into one. Betty nodded, as if solidifying herself. As head nurse, she had done this before, but it never got any easier.

Tess saw the look and knew in an instant what it meant. She knew before Ruth did and her heart broke.

Ruth's eyebrows furrowed, confused, and bewildered. Betty was definitely looking at her, but what was wrong? Had she made a mistake with a patient? With the paperwork that was often delegated to her by the senior nurses? Was Betty upset with her for the small talk with Tess?

"Ruth?" Betty said gently. "I need to see you, dear."

That was when Ruth knew that something was wrong, terribly wrong. Betty never called the others by their first name in the ward. And she definitely never called them "dear." Ruth's heart sank and a sweat popped out on her brow.

Ruth made her way to Betty, a short walk in

actual space but one that seemed to be forever and in slow motion. The senior nurse put an arm around Ruth's shoulders and guided her out of the ward. She stopped in the hallway, which was surprisingly empty.

"I've got terrible news for you. There's no easy way to say it, but your brother, Frank, has been killed in action. I'm so sorry, dear." Betty watched Ruth, knowing that the shock would dull an initial reaction but not for how long. She thought to herself that she should have led Ruth farther away from the ward. It wouldn't be good for the boys who were recovering to hear Ruth crying. No one needed any more reminders of death.

Ruth stared at Betty. She fixated on Betty's army insignia. The words she had just heard hung in the air. Maybe if she didn't respond, didn't react, Ruth thought, maybe it wouldn't be true. Her brother couldn't be dead, he just couldn't. Not brave, handsome Frank. Ruth's eyes burned with unshed tears.

Suddenly, two medics appeared in the hallway, nearly running as they carried a man on a gurney. "Casualty, Nurse," one medic said when he saw her. "Bad one. Leg blown off and he's lost a lot of blood." The latter comment was unnecessary. The unfortunate soul was leaving a trail of bright red spatters in his wake.

Ruth and Betty both took in the sight, one so familiar to them both. Betty's body reflexively moved toward the men, ready to aid the patient. She had taken a half-step when she froze and grabbed Ruth by both arms. "I'm sorry, dear." With that, she was gone, following the medics toward the operating theatre. There were more soldiers to take care of and nothing could be done for the dead man who was Ruth's brother.

Ruth watched Betty go and allowed her mind to wonder if the new casualty would survive. She wondered where he had come from and how he would fit into her map of the United States. She stood there, immobilized. After a few moments, her brain refused to allow her an escape as it began processing the horrible news.

How did Frank die? Was his leg blown off, too? Had he suffered? The reality of the news slowly began to sink in. He was gone. Gone like the scores of men that Ruth had seen come into the hospital with at least a chance but left covered with a white sheet. She had been so sure that Frank would be safe. After all, he was her big brother, invincible and brave. Ruth could feel her heart pounding in her ears as the realization that Frank would never be going home, that they would never share stories of their time in the war, crept into her consciousness. She felt a shiver of panic as the psychic pain began to settle in.

And then, Tess was there. She wrapped Ruth in her arms. "Your brother?" she asked softly.

Ruth could only nod.

"Oh, my love. I'm so sorry. Come with me." Tess led a dazed Ruth through the hospital corridor and to the bunkroom. Ruth followed, in a daze of unreality.

The bunkroom was fairly quiet, with only a few nurses off shift, some sleeping, some reading, and some writing letters. They all looked up when Ruth entered and, seeing the devastation of her face, looked away quickly, out of respect for her privacy. They knew from experience that the news was too raw.

"Lie down, now," Tess whispered.

Ruth obediently complied, still silent. She closed

her eyes but as soon as she did so, all she could see was her brother. The images came quickly and without pause, almost like a movie. Frank as a young boy, reaching a hand down to help Ruth into the treehouse. Frank as a high school athlete. Frank sitting on his bed, talking as he packed his trunk to join the Army. Frank in a firefight, ducking and firing a weapon. She would never see Frank again, she realized, except in memories or photographs. She kept her eyes closed despite the pain but sleep was not to be hers for many hours.

Ruth's eyes were nearly swollen shut. She had alternated between sobbing and dozing in short bits of fitful sleep, ruined with nightmares. Each time she woke, she experienced the pain of realization anew. Her brother was dead. The hours of crying had offered no solace, no release. Tess had climbed into her bed with her, not worrying about the other nurses, not worrying about Helene. No one had thought anything of it, other than pity and sorrow for one of their sisters, mourning the abrupt loss of her brother. It was a scene played out too often, brothers, husbands, boyfriends, so many lost. Each woman who saw Ruth in her misery was privately hoping it wouldn't happen to her. It wasn't cruel or thoughtless; it was war.

Tess's arms had felt so welcome to Ruth. Her soft murmurs of comfort, her hand stroking Ruth's hair. In the midst of the pain, Ruth felt a swell of gratitude that she had found this woman. How could she have borne this painful moment without her? The "cold fish" was nothing of the sort.

"I have a shift; I have to go," Tess had whispered

to Ruth. Tess had waited as long as she could to leave Ruth's side. She had considered not saying good-bye as Ruth had finally drifted into a light sleep, but didn't want her to wake up and wonder why she was alone. A fierce sense of protectiveness, tenderness and, yes, love, swept through Tess while she had held Ruth through the long night. Something was changing between them and Tess was frightened. But now was not the time for those thoughts. Ruth needed her now.

"I wish you could stay," Ruth said, not opening her eyes. She tightened her grip on Tess, as if she could physically keep her close. She was finding herself addicted to simple caresses from Tess. When Helene had stroked her, usually after sex, the caresses felt more like the distracted touches that one would give a pet. When Tess touched her, Ruth could feel the infusion of warmth…and love.

"I wish I could, love. I'll be back." With a squeeze of her arms and a feather light kiss on Ruth's head, Tess gently extricated herself and left.

With the warmth and comfort of Tess now gone, Ruth's mind whirred into motion. She allowed a thought that had inserted itself in her head almost immediately after she heard the terrible news to develop. It was a thought for which she felt tremendous guilt. She gingerly tested the worry that was pushing and nagging her, the thought that was taking up space that Ruth believed should have been devoted to grief, to anguish. With Frank gone, how could she stay away from home? Her mother would be devastated at the loss of her son; now was the time that Ruth was needed. It was the only thing that she could do, the only thing any daughter could do.

Wasn't it?

Betty had found Ruth getting ready for a shift and shook her head. "No, Ruth. Take the day for yourself. You've had an awful shock." Her kind eyes held Ruth's. "No one expects you to return to duty immediately after losing someone."

"But I think it would help, Betty. I'm tired of thinking about what's happened. I just want to drown out the sadness. Doing a shift will let me focus on something positive." The truth was Ruth was emotionally and physically exhausted. She honestly didn't know if her body would carry her through an arduous shift in the ward. Just the same, she didn't know if her heart would carry her through eight more hours of thinking about her lost brother. Neither option was a good one.

Betty made the decision for her. "No, and that's an order. I can't have you on the ward when you're like this. You might make a mistake and it's not worth the risk. Things are relatively quiet over there and we can spare you. Trust me, hon, I've seen others go through this before. You think you can do it, but you need a bit of time to process." She gave Ruth a little hug. "Why don't you head over to the common room and relax? I think some of the girls are over there playing cards. Some company might do you good."

Grateful for the kindness of her friend and supervisor, Ruth nodded. "Maybe you're right."

"I know I am," Betty said with a warm smile. She patted Ruth's hand. "I'll see you soon."

Betty walked off, heading to another shift. Ruth watched her go. She knew Betty was one of the girls that she would never forget, no matter how old she grew. But of course, there was another woman here that would always have a place in Ruth's heart.

※ ※ ※ ※

Betty had been right. A handful of nurses playing cards and another sitting at a table, writing a letter, occupied the common room. When Ruth walked in, their chatter stopped. Each looked up at Ruth, their faces a mirror of their thoughts. *Poor Ruth. I heard it was her brother. I hope we don't have another notification anytime soon.*

Several of them got up right away and converged on Ruth, enveloping her in a mass hug.

"We're so sorry, honey," they were saying. There wasn't much else to say. The scene had been repeated many times among the nurses but it never got any easier.

Ruth allowed herself to surrender to the embraces and felt the warmness of her friends. It made her feel better, she had to admit, and she was glad that she had taken Betty's advice and sought out company.

"Want to play a hand with us?" Delilah asked. "It'll take your mind off of things."

"I think I'll just watch," Ruth responded. She pulled up a chair and settled back, grateful to let her mind drift.

An easy hour had passed, with the women engaging in light chatter and bragging about their poker hands, when one of them asked the question that had been burning in Ruth's mind.

"So, Ruth, will you go home now?"

Delilah shot a glare at the woman but then looked

at Ruth. She was curious, too.

"I've been thinking about that," Ruth said, stalling.

"I know I would go, if it were me," Ruby said with her characteristic Texas twang. "If mama and daddy lost Beau, they'd be almost beyond repair. Course Beau is deaf in one ear and is still at home so I'll never have to deal with that." She looked up, realizing too late that she had become insensitive in her chatter. "Sorry, Ruthie."

Ruth shrugged. "It's okay. It seems the same. My parents, I mean. They adored Frank." The use of past tense about her brother felt foreign in her mouth. "I don't know how they'll survive this. It seems selfish if I don't go home."

Her words came out as a statement but really, they were a question. The question wasn't directed to the friendly nurses, but inward. Would she be able to live with herself if she left her parents to suffer alone in Indiana? Was it selfish? If it was selfish, was it okay to want to be here with Tess, to be happy?

The women felt the awkwardness of the moment and Ruby recovered for her transgression by moving the conversation past the road bump. "Let's have another hand, ladies."

Ruth threw Ruby a grateful smile and leaned back in her chair. She watched the next hand, with the pot going to Delilah, and was about to say that she would play after all when she saw Tess in the doorway of the room. She walked over to meet her lover, vaguely aware of the nurses' reaction. Most of them knew about the relationship, primarily because of proximity of bunks. Whatever their personal feelings, each felt a tug at their heart—they knew Ruth and Tess were facing a challenge.

"I looked for you in the bunkroom but you weren't there," Tess said. "I was hoping you weren't pulling a shift."

"I had to get out of there, away from my own thoughts, if that makes sense."

"It does." Tess touched Ruth's face, a gentle brush that spoke volumes. "I imagine your mind is quite busy. I wish there was something I could do to help."

"I know." An awkward silence settled in. The proverbial elephant in the room was present.

"I suppose you've been thinking about whether to stay or go," Tess said at last.

Ruth could only nod.

"I'll support your decision no matter what, love." Tess's eyes were kind but there was a sadness behind them. It was as if she were steeling herself for another round of pain.

"Thank you. I think I just need some time to think about it."

In the end, it took only two days.

Chapter Twenty-three

"You've decided." Tess's words were not a question.

"Yes." Ruth couldn't look at her lover. It was too hard. She knew that she was causing Tess pain and of the worst sort. It would be a familiar pain, one that Tess had already endured, one that she had tried to protect herself against ever feeling again. Until, that is, Ruth had promised her that she could trust her and swore that she never had to worry about Ruth leaving her. Except, that was what Ruth was doing—leaving her. Not by choice, not by any means, but by a deep sense of obligation, which guilt further fueled. "I'm sorry."

The words were useless, both knew. But what else was there to say?

Numerous other conversations were taking place in the bar, but none like this one. The women sat across from one another at a table, possibly even the same table where they had shared their first drink together. Each fidgeted with her beer, both sitting untouched.

"When will you go?" Tess's voice had taken on the curt, efficient tone and cadence that Ruth had known when the Englishwoman first arrived. Gone was the softness that Tess had used when whispering to Ruth at night, telling her that she loved her, and cruelly now in retrospect, that she trusted her.

It was the broken trust that Ruth felt most

sharply. Her guts twisted with distress and anguish. For an instant, she wished that she had already gone, that she was already aboard the ship that would take her back to the States. At least then, Ruth could try to forget about this woman that she was leaving behind. If she didn't have to see Tess, with her jaw tightened against emotion and her brown eyes flashing with poorly concealed pain, perhaps Ruth could stop the heartache that she was feeling. But she wasn't at sea. She was in the tiny bar across from the woman she loved.

"Within the week, Betty says." Ruth's voice broke as she spoke. There was so much that she wanted to say. She swallowed against the painful lump in her throat. "Tess, I want you to know how hard it was to—"

"No need," Tess injected, still with the empty tone. "I understand. Really, I do. It's the right thing to do."

Hearing her lover try to let her off of the hook, without words of hurt or recrimination, made Ruth feel even worse. How could she do this to Tess? And to herself? Hadn't they been so fortunate to have found one another? How could she leave just when her life seemed to be beginning? Doubt crowded Ruth's mind and before she could make sense of it, she spoke again. "But I don't want to leave," she said, her voice breaking again. "I don't want to leave you. Maybe I can just stay here; Mom has Dad after all."

Tess looked at Ruth at last. Her heart wanted desperately to tell Ruth yes! Yes, stay here. Let your parents get on by themselves. But Tess wasn't that kind of person. Her eyes said everything but she spoke nonetheless. "Don't be silly. You should be home. Your parents have suffered a grievous loss. It would be selfish of you, of us, to deprive them of their daughter, to keep her in harm's way."

Ruth laid her hand on Tess's. It was warm and soft, even with the constant hand-washing of a wartime nurse. "But I love you."

Tess closed her eyes and appeared to be trying to collect herself. She covered Ruth's hand with her own. "I know. And I love you. It's why I must tell you to go. I don't want you here out of guilt or obligation."

Ruth began to cry, tears dripping quickly from her eyes without a sound. She shook her head, overcome. The moment was the most painful she had ever known.

"Perhaps after the war, you'll come back. Or, I could come to America. I've always wanted to see it, you know." Tess was trying valiantly to make the moment easier on them both. But both knew that such a trip would never happen. It was unlikely that either woman would make the trans-Atlantic journey. And what if Tess did go to the States? Would they be able to share a life together? They were trapped in a hopeless situation and they both were acutely aware of the fact that their days together were numbered.

※ ※ ※ ※

The next night, after Ruth had surreptitiously extracted the key from Helene's footlocker, she led Tess to the quiet, vacant corridor of doctor's offices. After unlocking the door, Ruth looked back at Tess.

"Wait here for a minute."

Tess nodded and watched Ruth disappear inside with the bag she had been carrying. A few moments later, she was back. Ruth held out a hand and beckoned Tess into the room.

The small office had been made as romantic as was possible, given the circumstances. Several candles were lit, casting a warm, pleasant glow over the mattress, which a clean, white sheet covered. From somewhere, Tess didn't want to know how, Ruth had managed to secure a bottle of wine.

Ruth looked at Tess, shyly waiting for her reaction.

"It's lovely," Tess said, squeezing Ruth's hand. "Just lovely."

Both knew that their time together was ending. Both knew that this night could very well be their last together. It was too painful to comment on the fact and they somehow resolved, without discussion, not to talk about the specialness of the night or to dissolve into sorrow. Tonight was for love.

"Relax, kick off your shoes," Ruth said, as she did the same.

Tess removed her shoes and heavy socks and wiggled her toes.

"Even your toes are beautiful," Ruth said.

"You're a sweet talker, aren't you?"

"I don't know about that. I do know that I love you," Ruth said, her voice full of emotion.

"And I know that your love has set me free. You've given me the greatest gift."

The moment was full and the air between the women felt warm and soft. The world outside vanished and it was just them, an Englishwoman and an American, two souls who somehow found one another in the most unlikely of settings.

Ruth guided Tess to the mattress and the women dissolved immediately into a kiss. Their mouths met with a familiarity that exceeded their time together but matched their intimacy. With tongues darting in between mouths and full lips upon full lips, the energy between them began to build.

Tess gripped Ruth's auburn hair, pulling her closer. Responding to Tess's motion, Ruth moaned.

"I love that sound," Tess murmured. She leaned away from Ruth, just far enough to allow her room to pull Ruth's blouse over her head. When Ruth reached to unclasp her bra, Tess stopped her. "Let me."

With one finger, Tess slid a strap from Ruth's shoulder and then the other. Looking into her lover's eyes, she unfastened the closure and removed the bra, dropping it on the mattress beside them. Staring at Ruth's breasts, Tess smiled before caressing them. Ruth's body quickly responded to the touch, her nipples becoming hard rosebuds in Tess's hands. When Tess dipped down to take a breast in her mouth, Ruth threw her head back and arched her back.

Tess sucked gently at first, then harder as she felt Ruth reacting. She flicked at the nipple with her tongue, alternating quick licks and slow, leisurely circles. Not wanting to neglect the other breast, Tess continued to massage Ruth.

"Now you. I want to see you," Ruth said, breathlessly. She pulled Tess's top from her and made quick work of the brassiere. For Ruth, there was no slow tease. She couldn't make herself. Instead, she pushed Tess gently, urging her to lie on her back. Climbing on top of the Englishwoman, Ruth held both of Tess's breasts, giving them a squeeze before positioning her mouth over one. Tess's full breast barely fit into Ruth's mouth but she enjoyed the challenge. She rolled Tess around in her mouth, sucking her erect nipple. Removing her mouth, she ran a slow circle around

Tess with her tongue, moving ever-inward towards the waiting nipple, which she licked with abandon. As she moved, she looked up at Tess.

Tess was watching intently, her brown eyes flashing with arousal. "It's as if you're devouring me," Tess said in a throaty voice. "I love it."

Ruth responded with action, not words. She sat up, pulled Tess's skirt down, and carefully maneuvered it off. The cotton underwear came next, with Tess lifting her hips slightly to help Ruth. Ruth then stood up, her feet between Tess's outstretched legs, and deftly removed her own trousers and underwear. She began to kneel back down when Tess spoke.

"Wait. Just stand there for a moment and let me look at you."

Ruth did as Tess asked and stood straight and tall over her prone lover. In that moment, Ruth felt a powerful pride in her naked body, in her womanhood. She was coursing with desire and her body was buzzing with a forceful reaction to this beautiful, nude woman who lay before her. She was so thankful to be "one of those girls." Anything that made her feel like this was a gift and in that time and that place, Ruth knew she had found herself. She would deal with the heartache that she knew she was coming tomorrow. Tonight, she was happy.

"You're exquisite, you know that?" Tess said quietly. Her eyes took in every inch of Ruth's body.

Ruth smiled. Still reveling in the high of the moment, she ran a finger down the middle of her chest to her stomach. Seeing Tess's expression, her eyes now narrowed with lust, Ruth continued, emboldened by the approval. She took her own breasts in her hands and rubbed them, squeezing her nipples as she watched

Tess watching her.

"Keep going," Tess whispered, mesmerized.

Ruth touched herself between her legs, tracing a line through her sex. The contact caused her to gasp. With two fingers, she rubbed her growing clit, the sensation sending streaks of pleasure throughout her. Just as exciting as the pressure between her legs was seeing Tess, her eyes glued to Ruth and her own hands now straying to her body to give attention where it was so desperately needed.

Unable to resist her lover's body any longer, Ruth lowered herself to the mattress and came to rest with her mouth between Tess's waiting legs. She could see that Tess was excited, her wet openness inviting her in. Sinking into Tess's sex, Ruth had an overwhelming feeling of contentment. Although her body was aching for relief, her soul was full. This was where she belonged, pleasing this wonderful woman, free from any feelings of insecurity or distrust. Ruth wished the experience could have lasted forever. She felt as if she were in a hazy trance of joy, her mouth on Tess, tasting her, her tongue inside of the slick warmth, feeling Tess's hands in her hair and then Tess's legs at her head, urging her on. When Tess reached her climax and cried out with release, Ruth stayed in place, teasing her and pushing her farther with her tongue. They were both rewarded, Tess with a second wave of ecstasy and Ruth with a rush of warmth in her mouth.

Ruth stayed between Tess's legs, watching her face as she let the last surges of pleasure wash over her. Her eyes were closed and her face was peaceful. Ruth slid up Tess's strong body and kissed her.

Tess's eyes opened. "I taste myself," she said.

With a smile, Ruth nodded and returned

her mouth to Tess's. Tess's peaceful countenance evaporated as another swell of desire took over. She rolled over, placing Ruth beneath her and spread Ruth's legs with her own. Reaching down, she felt Ruth's slippery swollenness and groaned. With a quick push, she was inside of Ruth, two fingers, then three. Ruth's eyes opened wide and then closed again as she let her legs rest open, surrendering herself to Tess.

Tess responded immediately, thrusting again and again into Ruth, delighting in the warm suction that grabbed greedily at her fingers each time.

Ruth moaned as she arched her hips, demanding without words that Tess continue.

Tess nipped Ruth's breast gently, feeling the impossible hardness of her nipple as she continued to push in and out of her partner. When Ruth began to moan rhythmically, she pressed her thumb on Ruth's clitoris, easily finding its stiffness. The contact sent Ruth into earthquakes of pleasure and her moans grew louder. Tess flicked her thumb back and forth as rapidly as she could move and made her strokes shorter and stronger. Ruth arched even higher into Tess's hand, desperately needing everything that she was giving. When she cried out at the moment of her orgasm, Tess's name echoed in the small room.

The intensity of their lovemaking was so pronounced that it was like a third person with them. Both were acutely aware of the suddenly very finite time that they had together. Both wanted to extract every molecule of closeness possible in the time they had left. They dared not speak of it, lest the magic be stolen.

"I'll never forget this night," Ruth said at last, her face buried in Tess's neck.

Tess looked up at the ceiling, shadows cast and flickering from the shrinking candles. She wanted to say so many things, but the die had been cast. A practical Englishwoman, she knew some things were simply out of one's control. "Nor will I, love. Nor will I."

Chapter Twenty-four

The sound was so loud that Ruth, even with her wartime-acquired ability to tune out loud noises, was jarred awake. The other nurses in the bunkroom were also stirring, sitting up in their beds and chattering.

"What was that?"

"Is everyone okay?"

"Now the air raid sirens are going!"

It was true; the droning squeal of the air raid sirens filled the air, their see-sawing drone sickeningly real and not a test. Being nurses, the women immediately began throwing on uniforms and heading out to assist, even though most had just come off of a long shift.

Ruth looked at her trunk, pushed against her bed and ready for her departure later that day. She had packed all of her uniforms but knew she couldn't stand idly by when she could help. This would be her last chance and she didn't want to go home knowing that she could have done more. With a glance at Tess's empty bed, Ruth also knew that part of her reason for wanting to get to the operating room and triage was to see Tess, even for a few more moments. Despite their agreement to finish their good-byes the previous night, Ruth couldn't resist the pull.

Triage was pure chaos. All hands seemed to be on deck, with doctors and nurses virtually bumping into each other as they rushed to tend to the desperately injured. There were so many gurneys in the area that the medical personnel were literally stepping over bodies.

"Where's Tess?" Ruth asked Midgie as they worked together to stop a patient's bleeding. She had pulled on a mask and gloves almost without stopping.

"Tess? She should be coming in with this load. I know she went out early this morning to help the boys with field triage. Haven't seen her yet. Good luck, honey. Write me." Midgie looked tired but gave Ruth a smile before she rushed to the next patient.

Ruth's heart sank. She suddenly had a bad feeling and wished she hadn't left the bunkroom. Perhaps if she hadn't left the bunkroom, none of this would be happening. Two medics carrying a wounded man on a gurney pushed by. Ruth recognized one of them.

"Harry! Tess, Nurse Davies I mean. Is she with you?"

"Haven't seen her since earlier this morning, sweetheart." The words were no sooner spoken than Harry and his counterpart were gone, carrying their charge directly to a table in the operating room.

Ruth shook her head, trying to clear it of the images that were coming unbidden. *Please be safe*, she thought. She looked down at the patient she was helping with and toward the door. *I need to find her.* "Can you finish this one?" she asked the other nurse.

The other woman barely looked up. Fluidity of treatment was one of the hallmarks of wartime nursing. "Sure."

Ruth backed away from the patient. She looked

at him briefly, a dark-haired young man with a terrible belly wound. *I'm sorry*, she told him silently. Peeling off her gloves and mask as she went, Ruth hurried out of the operating room.

The world outside of the OR was no less chaotic. Sirens continued to blare and the din of the hospital went unchecked. Wounded men groaned or shouted, doctors snapped orders, nurses rushed from patient to patient. But Ruth saw the hospital through a haze of disinterest. She needed to get out of there and find Tess. She couldn't leave this country, this war, without knowing Tess was okay.

The street was a site of unbelievable destruction. Piles of smoking rubble dotted the landscape, punctuated by civilians helping one another get to a safer place. Ruth saw several stray dogs, hopelessly confused and sniffing frantically for food, or maybe their owners. Ruth knew the likelihood of them finding either was slim. But that couldn't distract her now. She had to find Tess.

A flash of white caught Ruth's eye. A nurse's cap? She felt a smile forming as she moved forward and yelled out. "Tess!"

The woman under the cap turned…but it wasn't Tess. Ruth didn't recognize the nurse. Ruth felt her heart sink into her stomach. She approached the stranger. "Sorry, I thought you were someone else. I'm looking for a nurse, Tess Davies. An Englishwoman. Have you seen her?"

"I'm sorry, love, I don't know her." The other woman's English accent was a reminder of Tess. "But I did see a medical group move off in that direction." She gestured to the west.

Ruth grabbed the nurse's arm, grateful for any

shred of hope that she might find Tess. "Thank you!" With that, she raced off, squinting against the sun that bore witness to so many tragedies, only to rise again the next day.

The going was rocky, the streets strewn with rubble and nearly impassable in some spots. Several small fires sputtered. Ruth moved as quickly as she could, too quickly it turned out. She tripped over a storefront sign that had been knocked from its frame and went sprawling.

Sitting up, Ruth assessed the damage. She had scraped her hands and forearms and she could see ground debris had lodged itself in her skin. She ignored the sting and examined her ankle, which had caught the sign and caused the fall in the first place. It was already swelling and she knew from the pain that she must have sprained it, badly. Her eyes filled with tears, not from pain, but from frustration. She couldn't afford to be slowed down. She had to find Tess.

Hoisting herself to a standing position, Ruth gingerly put weight on the twisted ankle and the lightning bolt of pain confirmed her self-diagnosis. *Damn,* she cursed. Walking slowly, she hobbled forward, looking everywhere for the woman she loved. *Please God,* she prayed, *let her be okay.* She covered several blocks, her ankle screaming in agony as she walked. The abrasions in her hands and forearms made themselves known as well, beginning to throb. Tears flowed down her face as she looked frantically for Tess.

Finally, up ahead, Ruth recognized one of the nurses from the hospital. It was Shorty. She must have been on the triage with Tess! Ignoring the white-hot pain, Ruth broke into a jog to reach Shorty.

Shorty was kneeling over a patient in the middle

of the road, a woman whose head was covered in blood. She worked efficiently and quickly alongside a medic.

"Shorty!" Ruth called.

Shorty looked up, surprised to hear her name in this setting. When she saw Ruth, she half-smiled and nodded. "Ruth! You here to help? We could use it."

Ruth ignored the question. "Tess. Have you seen Tess?"

Shorty shook her head. "No, not since we left. Can you help me with this bleeder?"

Ruth stared at Shorty. She had been so sure that Shorty was going to tell her that Tess was on her way back to the hospital or that Tess was the next block over and she was fine. She backed away, as if physical distance might change the answer.

"You mean Davies?" the medic asked as he worked on the injured woman without looking up.

A swell of hope surged through Ruth. "Yes! Davies, Tess Davies. You've seen her?"

"I'm sorry, sweetheart. She's missing. She didn't catch check-in with the last group and I just heard on our radio that we need to keep an eye out. Not that we don't already have our hands full." The medic didn't miss a beat with his treatment as he talked.

Ruth ignored the medic's last comment. All she heard was two words. She's missing. She's missing. She continued to back away from Shorty and the medic and kept moving, Shorty's words in the distance.

"Ruth? We need your help. Come back!"

Ruth ran until the pain in her ankle grew too excruciating. She felt a wave of nausea and her head had begun to throb. She had no idea how far she had gone or even where she was. It didn't matter now. She sat on a mangled curb, not caring that her uniform was growing filthy in the street.

It was the last straw. Ruth felt a gnawing dread in her gut. The growing pit in her stomach was like a crystal ball. She knew in her heart that Tess wasn't just missing. Tess was gone just like Frank, just like Gabriel, and just like so many others. How could life be so cruel as to put she and Tess together, to give them a whisper of the possibility of a life together, only to snatch it away? What had either of them done to deserve that? *If only I had told her I would stay*, Ruth thought miserably. *Then she wouldn't have left, wouldn't have gone on this field triage. It's my own fault for being a coward and not living my own life.*

With her head in her hands, she cried. She cried for the loss of Gabriel, the loss of her brother, the loss of her innocence, and most of all, she cried for Tess. Heaving sobs of despair tore from her, each more desperate than the last. She felt the hot sting of her tears as they coursed down her face and tasted the salt of each. The tears brought no relief, no sense of cleansing, though, and Ruth knew they were far from the last.

Ruth sat on the curb, another victim of the war who lived. She wasn't sure how long she had been there, keening and hurting, before she felt a hand on her shoulder. Looking up through swollen eyes, she squinted. The figure was silhouetted in sunshine so bright that it took Ruth a moment to make out whether the figure was a man or a woman.

It was a woman. It was Tess.

Tess stood in front of Ruth, her eyes a mix of happiness and surprise. A fresh cut marked her left cheek and her hair was a mess, but it was Tess. Alive and safe. The two women stared at one another, each taking stock of the situation and ensuring that it was reality.

"You...you're alive," Ruth said, still not believing what she was seeing.

Tess knelt beside Ruth so that they were face to face. "Of course I'm alive. And you, you're here. I thought you'd left for...home."

"I wanted to see you one more time," Ruth said, her voice cracking. "They said you'd gone out and seeing what the bombing did, I thought, I thought—"

"There, there, my love. I'm fine. Look at me, I'm safe and sound and right here. I got separated from the team. I was working with them when a little girl saw me and begged me to help her mother. She couldn't have been more than four, such a brave little one. She said she was having a baby and the baby wouldn't come." Tess sat on the curb, holding Ruth's arm.

"A baby," Ruth murmured, still stunned at the appearance of the woman who she had felt sure was gone forever.

"Yes. I told the medics I'd be right back, to wait for me. But, by the time I got back, they were gone. I'm sure they had to take some wounded back to the hospital. I knew I'd find them eventually or make my way back to the hospital on my own. But the baby, Ruth..." Tess paused to take a breath.

Ruth held Tess's hand, warm and strong. She gripped it as if she was afraid that if she didn't keep a hand on this woman, she would vanish into thin air. Trying to focus on what Tess was saying, she had a sinking feeling she knew how this story would end. It seemed to be the ending to all too many stories these days. "It didn't survive?"

Tess kissed Ruth square on the mouth, ebullient.

"No! It did survive. She did, I mean. It was a breech and difficult to get through but the woman delivered a healthy baby girl. Here, in the midst of all of this, she delivered a beautiful little girl. That baby fought to be born and came into this world with a yell so loud that even I was startled." Tess's eyes filled with happy tears. "There is hope, after all."

In that moment, both women knew. They knew that they were meant to be together. Not time or distance or attitudes could keep them apart. Here too, in the midst of the living hell of war, they had found each other for a reason. How could they possibly deny the miracle of that? They looked at each other, communicating wordlessly, smiles forming as they realized what was happening.

"You're staying then?" Tess asked. But she already knew the answer.

"I'm staying. With you."

Epilogue

Evansville, Indiana 1963

The Carroway house looked a little worse for wear, having stood solid for nearly twenty years since World War II. The victory garden was still there, but they no longer called it a victory garden. Instead, it was Neil's pride and joy. He entered his famously large pumpkins in the state fair every year and had been a runner-up twice. Every new year brought his proclamation that "this was his year."

He was carrying a bag of yard clippings to the curb when he caught sight of a teenage girl bicycling down the street. He waved and smiled when the pretty blonde-haired girl waved back. It was little Ruth Reed from two streets over. Her mother, Lillian, had remarried after the war, to a nice fellow who ran the local hardware store. The Carroways had all been pleased to learn that she was naming her baby girl after her good friend, Ruth. It was hard to believe that had been fifteen years ago. Where did the time go? Neil liked Lillian and the new husband, Hank, but always thought that the woman looked sad, despite her smiles.

Neil stopped at the mailbox and then returned inside, careful not to let the door slam. Mary was always a little edgy and Neil tried to keep things as calm as he could for her. She had never been the same after the war, after the loss of Frank. It had been ten years before

Neil was able to convince Mary to remove the shrine to their boy and another year after that before she finally agreed to change his boyhood room to a sewing room.

"That way you can relax and enjoy the room and still honor Frank," Neil had said, trying to placate his wife while still dealing with his own, ever-present loss.

He found Mary in the kitchen, peeling apples for a pie. "I've got something exciting," Neil said, waving an envelope with now familiar red and blue borders.

Mary wiped her hands on a towel and smiled a broad smile. The smile lifted Neil's heart, as it always did. There had been a time right after the war when he'd thought he might lose Mary to her grief. Thankfully, time and peace had helped her heal.

"Is that what I think it is?" Mary asked, pulling on her eyeglasses, which hung from a chain around her neck.

"It sure is. Here, sit down." Neil pulled a chair out for his wife and pushed it in slightly after she had taken a seat. He looked around and frowned.

"Looking for your glasses?" Mary asked. Seeing him nod in the affirmative, she gently pulled them from the top of his head to the bridge of his nose. "You never remember," she said with a gentle laugh.

Neil kissed his wife on the cheek and then carefully opened the envelope, treating the thin paper as if it were a treasure. To Mary and Neil, it was.

❧ ❧ ☙ ☙

Dear Mother and Pop,

I hope this finds you well! I can't believe that it's October already, can you? I do miss the changing leaves this time of year. London doesn't have that, I'll tell you.

    Things here are same as ever. Busy as can be at the hospital. In between teaching the nursing classes and serving as supervisor, I feel that the days fly by. That's a good thing, right Pop? I remember you telling me that hard, honorable work was a blessing. I completely agree.

    Tess and I took a short holiday to France earlier this month. I am lucky to have found a roommate who likes to travel as much as I do. We ate more cheese and drank more wine than you can imagine. Mother, you would have loved seeing the cathedrals there, they were simply beautiful. When I get my photographs developed I will make sure to send you some of the best ones. That Brownie camera that you sent sure came in handy.

    You asked last time you wrote if I still hear from the nurses I met during the war. I do. A group of us write back and forth fairly often and it's always nice to hear from them. Some days it feels as if it were only yesterday that I was that scared young girl in London. The girls' letters always make me feel that way, even though we are certainly no longer girls! We always talk of trying to meet up, a reunion of sorts, and I hope that happens.

    I'll close here as Tess and I are going to go for a bicycle ride. She sends her best as always as do I.

    Love,
    Ruth

About the Author

Rachel Windsor is a boring attorney who enjoys writing in her free time. To spice up her day job of drafting appellate briefs, pension plans and tax documents, she writes lesbian fiction, romantic comedies, historical romance and erotica. Although she never achieved her childhood dream of becoming an astronaut, she thinks she ended up with a pretty cool life.

In addition to writing, Rachel enjoys spending time with her wife and their two children, traveling, enjoying good food and wine, and reading.

Contact info:
Facebook: facebook.com/rachel.windsor.560
Author website: rachelwindsor.com

Check out Rachel's other books.

Best Lesbian Erotica - ISBN - 978-1-943353-15-6

Lusty and Fun

Better set aside some "me time" once you have your hands on this award-winning collection of hot, sheet-twisting erotic stories that will leave you squirming.

With group sex, first times, exhibitionism, domination, and toys, this 2015 Golden Crown Literary Society Award Winner (Erotica) has something for every lover of lesbian erotica. These stories burn with details so vivid you'll swear you can see, hear, smell, taste, and feel the women loving women within.

Best Lesbian Erotica - It's the next best thing to being there.

This book was originally published as Best Lesbian Erotica 2014.

Lesbian Lovers Throughout Time Collection - ISBN - 978-1-943353-11-8

Enjor four stand-alone novellas in this 2015 Golden Crown Literary Society Finalist collection about women falling in love with each other throughout time.

Prairie Women in Love
It is hard being a woman in the 1870s and even harder if you happen to have feelings for another woman.

Civil War Women in Love
A plantation owner's daughter has to decide where her allegiance lies after falling in love with a house slave.

Dames with Dames
In 1940s New York City tough girl walks into a detective agency and things will never be the same for the agency's gorgeous secretary.

West Point Women in Love
At West Point in 1976, things are changing as the first female cadets arrive and even more so for two cadets as they face an undeniable attraction.

Love, Laughs and Lesbians - ISBN - 978-1-943353-13-2

Enjoy three stand-alone novellas in this collection of fiendishly funny, smart romantic comedies.

Mail Order Bride
Liz was ready to give up on love when a brainstorm hit—a mail order bride. The brainstorm becomes more than she bargained for when Svetlana arrives and utters those magical first words: "You are not man."

Gentlewomen Thieves
Joan's writing career has stalled out, along with her relationship with long-time partner Laura. Joan convinces Laura to embark on a live of crime to stir things up, leading to unexpected experiences for the couple.

Exit Row
Lauren hates to fly but hits it off with seatmate Natalie. Things get off to a rough start, literally, when their plane

nearly crashes. They impulsively get married and are asked to star on a reality show. Can they pull off their "feel-good" story?

Heat: A Collection of Lesbian Erotica - ISBN - 978-1-943353-45-3

If you're looking for a collection of lesbian erotica that will leave you so hot and bothered that you need a cold shower after reading, look no further. HEAT has some "sin"-tillating reads for every erotica lover.

Award-winning lesbian erotica author Rachel Windsor delivers another book filled with sexy stories that flesh out your secret fantasies and beyond. Always wondered about exploring with stranger sex? HEAT will take you there. Got a thing for military women? HEAT has you covered. Ever fantasized about a doctor appointment that takes a naughty turn? HEAT takes care of you. Stir in first times, toys, college girls, and make-up sex and HEAT has something to excite every lover of lesbian erotica.

HEAT-the name says it all.